The McAtrix Derided

When he's not being Robertski Brothers, Adam Roberts is A.R.R.R. Roberts, who wrote *The Soddit*, and sometimes he's just plain old Adam Roberts, who wrote *Salt*, *On*, *Stone*, *Park Polar*, *Jupiter Magnified*, *Polystom* and *The Snow*.

The McAtrix Derided

robertski brothers

GOLLANCZ
LONDON

The right of Adam Roberts to be identified as the
author of this work has been asserted by him in accordance
with the Copyright, Designs and Patents Act 1988.

First published in Great Britain in 2004 by
Gollancz
An imprint of the Orion Publishing Group
Orion House, 5 Upper St Martin's Lane,
London WC2H 9EA

Third impression 2004

A CIP catalogue record for this book is
available from the British Library

ISBN 0 575 07568 6

Typeset at The Spartan Press Ltd,
Lymington, Hants

Printed in Great Britain by
Clays Ltd, St Ives plc

www.orionbooks.co.uk

Part 1
The McAtrix Derided

Prelude

Everything is dark. Somewhere a phone rings: *brr-rr, brr-rr, brr-rr*. A wintry sound.

The receiver is lifted from its cradle. 'Hello?'

'Ah, hello! Our specialist assessors happen to be in your area conducting a survey for publicity purposes. Could I interest you in a free valuation for aluminium window frames and garage fittings?'

'It's' – wearily – 'the middle of the night.'

'Day or night, we're committed to bringing you value for money, efficiency, and a free slimline calculator. Our expert will provide a valuation entirely without charge. There's no obligation to buy, and no employee of this company will call.'

'How will they provide a valuation of my windows if they don't call?'

A silence. 'They, er, could do it from across the street.'

'Goodnight.'

The phone is replaced in its cradle, and only the dark remains.

*

The phone rings a second time. The receiver is taken more hurriedly from its cradle.

'Yes? What? What is it?'

'Mr Everyman?'

'Yes, yes who is this?'

'This is X?Xxcu92765b__uuihk@untraceable.com. FREE! FREE! XXX, TRIPLE X, XXX, GUARANTEED SEX! HOT HONEYS HOPE U'RE HARD!'

'I *beg* your pardon?'

'Would you like to increase your penis length to, *a*, fifteen inches, *b*, twenty-five inches, or *c*, no limit! No limit!'

'Who on earth would want a limitlessly long penis?'

'Our team of specialist Dutch penoplasty surgeons are standing by the phones, ready to take *your* call. HOT HONEYS!'

'How did you obtain this number?'

'Mr Everyman, there's a serious message here. There's a serious message. Are you ready to hear the serious message?'

And Everyman pauses. Because it is just possible that the message he has been waiting for, the message that has haunted his dreams, is being cunningly masked in all this gibberish. He says, 'I . . . may be. What is it?'

'Hot Honkies!'

'Hot *honkies*?'

'No, wait a mo, Hot homunculuses – ah, no.'

'What—'

'Homozygote!' barks the voice on the other end of the phone line. 'Homousian!' Suddenly the tone of the voice changes completely. A stern and unsettlingly mechanical speaker intones: 'This phone conversation has performed an illegal action and will be closed down. Non-fatal error at 348–552. Do you wish to de-bug? Yes, no, cancel?'

The line goes dead.

Gordon slumps back in his bed. Recently he has been getting the strangest phone calls. Sometimes he thinks the whole world is going mad around him.

The phone rings a third time. The receiver is snatched up sharply.

'What? What – what is it?'

'Er,' says the voice at the other end. 'Is Larry there?'

'Larry? No. I think you have a wrong number.'

'Hi – *Larry*?'

'You've dialled wrong.'

'Er . . . is that Larry?'

'*No.* I *think* you've dialled a wrong number.'

'Why did you answer, if the number was wrong?' snaps the voice.

The line goes dead.

*

Gordon Everyman gets out of bed and pads about his flat. He goes to the window.

Outside his flat it is snowing, soft flakes drifting downwards, unwavering, falling through the black sky in slow motion. The neon sign from the chemist's opposite gives the snow a sickly greenish tint. On this sign, the top spar of the final 'T' has become bent and dislodged after a cat jumped on it. It now resembles an 'E' more than it does a 'T', such that the shop appears to be offering 'all nite chemise'. But the light the sign puts out is strong, and very green. The snowflakes catch the illumination at strange angles, giving them the appearance of impenetrable hieroglyphs as they tumble through Gordon's field of view.

Gordon Everyman stands by his window and stares at the snow for a long time.

The phone rings again.

'Gordon Everyman?' says a voice at the other end. 'Warehouse Price Viagra Can Be Yours! Key your credit card number into the—'

He pulls the socket from the wall.

*

Next day, at work, Gordon asks Tim, who works at his office: 'You know how you get spam e-mails?'

'Sure,' says Tim. 'Everybody gets spam.'

'Did you ever get a spam phone call?'

'Spam on the *phone*?' says Tim, unbelievingly. 'How do you mean?'

'Just like spam, but on the phone.'

'Jesus, no. That's weird.'

Weird, Gordon thinks. Weird is it. But the more he contemplates the universe, the more it seems to be predicated not on gravity, not on the strong or weak atomic force, not on the wave–particle duality, but on the bizarre. Ironically, in thinking this, he was not far from the truth. Not far from the truth at all. Or, to be more precise, not far as the *crow* flies, although his actual journey to this truth would involve certain detours, roundabout routes, lengthy delays, leaves on the line, and a replacement bus service between Feltham and Hounslow. But he gets there in the end. That's the important thing.

Chapter 1
Gordon

And, weirdly, it turns out to be a love story after all, in the end.

You see, for Gordon, the biggest problem was women. Women troubled him. An attractive woman could reduce him to a gabbling wreck in moments. By 'an attractive woman' must be understood any woman Gordon found attractive; and the truth was he found *every* woman attractive, in one way or another, with the twin exceptions only of Princess Diana and Madelaine Albright. He didn't know why he didn't find Princess Diana attractive. He knew he was supposed to, but there was something in the combination of her rectilinear chin and her plughole eyes that turned him off. It didn't really matter, of course, since the Princess – being dead – was unlikely to swing into Gordon's social circle. But that left the rest of womankind, and when trying to talk to the rest of womankind he metamorphosed into a man drowning in spittle. It was embarrassing. It was more than embarrassing. It was

Nbarrassing. It was Zbarrassing, and you can't get any more barrassing than that.

He couldn't understand why he turned into such a drivelling idiot in the company of the female. He *loved* women: he loved the way they looked, the way their minds worked, the way they wore their clothes. He loved what they wore their clothes over. He yearned for a love connection: to have a partner, a girlfriend. Even a penpal. But it didn't seem to be destined for him.

Sometimes he would stand in front of his bathroom mirror and hold a shaving mirror to the side of his face to try and find out how he looked in profile. Straight black hair which he washed often; eyes not too close apart, not too far away from one another, a slightly W-shaped chin, it was all right. Wasn't it? But then he'd look again, and he'd know he was fooling himself. He was not a prepossessing individual. Indeed, he was so far from being prepossessing as to be pretty much postpossessing. He had, he knew (peering close in at the bathroom mirror), myriad open pores on his nose and cheeks, which gave his skin the consistency of pumice, and which in his moments of self-doubt made him think his face looked like it had been built by the same people who made the muppets. And his nose was not a good shape. It was aquiline, which is to say, wet, with a long white shaft coming down from his forehead and a nobbled double curvature at the end.

9

Sometimes he thought about plastic surgery. But plastic surgery belonged to plastic places like Hollywood. It wasn't an option if you lived in Feltham. And what if, he thought idly – what if there were something cheaper than plastic surgery? But what was cheaper than plastic? Cardboard surgery? Papier-mâché surgery?

He didn't like the sound of that.

Besides which he knew, of course, that his problem was not surgical. It was his manner, not his looks. He need only meet woman in the corridor at work, or waiting for the elevator, or queuing in the sandwich shop down the road, and his heart thrummed like a ringing mobile set on vibrate mode. He blushed like a ketchup factory on fire. He would feel a tight sense of constriction inside him, as if the presence of the woman were somehow squeezing him. Then, as if his internal organs were all made of sponge and had been dipped in some hot salt solution, that sense of being squeezed would result in sweat starting to flow from all his pores at once. He sweated like a drain. Not that drains sweat as such, not being mammalian, or indeed alive, but I'm sure you see the point I'm making.

The odd thing was that he really wasn't shy. His problem was something the reverse of shyness. He did not shrink away from social encounters – instead he plunged in, mouth flapping, words flying, and before he had time to think what it was he was saying he had blurted out something incredibly embarrassing. He didn't know why he did this; he only knew that he had torpedoed his chances of true love more times than he could remember by simply saying the wrong thing.

And so, still, somehow, 'it' didn't happen – his connection, his special love. Maybe fate was saving 'it' for some future date. If so, Gordon could only hope that fate was using efficient refrigeration, or at least some sort of vacuum-packing technology, or 'it' would long ago have started to go off and smell. As it was there was an inevitable belatedness to his attempts at a love life; whenever he broke through the crust of his own embarrassment to strike up a conversation with a woman, he discovered that she already had a boyfriend, or girlfriend; that she was already married, that she was already committed, that he was not only too late, but belate. But still he clung to the hope that one day he would meet Ms Right, *Mademoiselle Droit*, an *amour* in shining nightie.

One day, he told himself, she'll come.

:^0

Gordon worked as a database coordinator for a company based in Southwark. This is what a typical day involved for him: first he would commute by train from Feltham, where he lived, to Waterloo, thereafter walking to his enormous bookcase-shaped office block. He took the lift to the fifth floor, and stepped into the open-plan office of Southwark Database Coordination Consolidated. He sat in his chair and logged on. He spent twenty minutes sorting through his new e-mails. He picked his nose, surreptitiously, putting his face close to his keyboard so that his co-workers couldn't see him do it (or so he thought). He spun his chair all the way around on its metal stalk. He chatted to Tim, who had the cell across from his.

He spent most of his time on-line surfing the net, adding his opinion to chatrooms, checking out arcane websites, constructing a more impressive virtual persona for himself on-line. With characteristic British pessimism he told himself that there was no point in all this, that he was merely setting himself up for disappointment. But (as he quoted wryly to himself) if it weren't for his disappointments he wouldn't have any appointments at all.

He had tried to meet women via the internet, but he had not enjoyed a marked success. The closest he had come had been when he swapped e-mails and instant messages with a woman called Evelyn Mulholland whom he met via DotCompanions. After two weeks of correspondence he began to think that he had at last discovered a soulmate. They talked of meeting up. Wise to the ways of blind contacts, he made sure early on in their exchanges to ascertain the precise gender of his correspondent: <<Dear Evelyn.>> he typed. <<How are you? Work was boring

today. Hey, by the way, you *are* a chick, yeah?>> In reply to this message he received a jpg which loaded up to reveal a photo of a gorgeous, green-eyed, svelte-cheeked, blonde-haired, sweepingly curved woman in her mid-twenties. The picture carried the legend, 'To GORDON: FROM EVELYN, MILLION-DOLLAR BABE!' Thus reassured, Gordon agreed to meet Evelyn on the concourse at Waterloo for a lunch date. They were to recognise one another by the copies of *Database Coordinator Monthly* each promised to carry under their left arms. Gordon, stiff in a new jacket and wearing Sssexy For Men cologne (it had a picture of a cobra on the bottle label), waited for over an hour, checking every attractive blonde who came and went. It was a further twenty minutes before he could force himself to accept that the only other person in the station carrying the appropriate magazine was a grot-faced, saggy-jowled man in his forties. Summoning his courage he approached this gentleman.

'Excuse me . . . Evelyn, is it?'

'Gordon! Hello!'

The prolonged waiting period and anxiety of anticipation had greatly increased Gordon's innate querulousness. 'Ohhh you're a *geezer*,' he said, in his whiniest voice. 'Jesus, Evelyn, I *asked* you if you were a girl, and you sent me a picture of this blonde *honey*. Million-dollar babe, *you* said.'

'Yes, and the good news,' said Evelyn urgently, 'is that the surgery will almost certainly cost *considerably less* than a million dollars! A friend of mine took that same photo to a surgeon, and was quoted eight hundred thou for everything except the hair. And there's always wigs, right? There's this wiggery in Poland Street that—'

'Eight hundred *thou*?' interrupted Gordon. His face had sagged so as to resemble the classic theatrical mask of tragedy.

'That,' said Evelyn, pawing Gordon's shoulder, 'is surely *loose change* to a company director like you – four hundred employees, you said, with offices in London and Frankfurt.'

It is true to say that Gordon had thuswise embellished his own circumstances during their exchanges. But rather than confess to this he pulled himself up to his full height, said something incoherent about the betrayal of trust, and marched off. 'I thought it was *understood*,' wailed Evelyn behind him.

After that incident, Gordon fought shy of internet contacts. He did his job in the day, and sometimes went out with his workmates to the Chain Bar round the corner. He added to his collection of SF and horror DVDs. He ate a lot of takeaway Indian food. He visited his parents in their semi-detached East Staines house, two Sundays a month. He tried real life, but it wasn't especially edifying.

And so the internet drew him in again. It promised so much: a realm in which he could achieve anything he wanted, in which he could adopt any personality. In the web, he was tall, handsome, and – according to his own self-description – irresistible to women. He built up his on-line persona, choosing a name – Nemo – from an old *League of Extraordinary Gentlemen* comic he'd been reading. If Gordon were a nobody, then Nemo at least could be a somebody.

That's what he hoped.

(c:

When he first made e-contact with Thinity – or, more accurately, when Thinity made e-contact with *him* – he was, accordingly, cautious. He roamed chatrooms using his 'Nemo' alias, and boasted freely about his hacking abilities. His hacking abilities were, in truth, non-existent. He couldn't hack a computer. He couldn't hack a pocket calculator. He could barely hack a cough. But in the virtual world of chatrooms and internet sites, embarrassments like truth could be blithely disregarded.

He typed furiously, into the night, grinning to himself. <<I've been hacking since I was ten. I've got inside the IRS. I peeked in the military intranets of seven major nations.>>

The woman with the cognomen Thinity seemed

interested. They swapped messages on a regular basis. 'Let's meet,' he texted. 'I don't think so,' she replied. 'Oh go on,' he texted. 'No,' she replied.

And that, he thought, was that. Probably best that way, he thought. 'She' is probably a hairy-legged bloke anyway, he thought.

In all three of these thoughts he was wrong.

Chapter 2

'I'm on the Train'

And so, one grey morning much like any other, Gordon clambered on to the 7:57 Waterloo train at Feltham station. He wasn't expecting anything out of the ordinary to happen.

Miraculously he found himself not one but two adjacent seats, which he claimed in the traditional manner by slumping in one and putting his tote bag on the other. Stretching his arms to open his newspaper wide effectively screened the little area from the other commuters. He rifled the pages until, passing world news and home news, he came to that part of the paper where the broadsheet reproduced tabloid scandal under the guise of critiquing it. The train trundled into motion, and he started reading the paper.

Lost to the world in this manner, it was a while before he became aware that somebody was standing over him. It was a woman. A woman in tight-fitting, black plastic trousers.

'Nemo?' said the woman.

Gordon dropped the paper to his lap. The speaker possessed a clear, well-modulated American-accented voice. She may have had a beautiful face. She could, indeed, have been very beautiful altogether. Gordon couldn't tell. He couldn't tell because he simply couldn't remove his gaze from the portion of tight-fitting trousers directly in front of his eyes. His line of sight was completely occupied by two thighs. Not only were these very shapely thighs, very shapely thighs *indeed*, but they were wrapped in close-tailored plastic, sheer, sheen, black, very tight. The plastic gripped the hips of the woman with an insolent closeness. It hugged her crotch, and by doing so it pushed into Gordon's mind the thought of a sentence in which the words 'hugged' and 'crotch' appeared of necessity in close proximity. These trousers looked inked on. They did not say 'workwear', or 'easyclean', or 'designer', or 'expensive', or any of those concepts. They said only two things: 'shapely leg here' and 'here's another'.

Gordon's mouth had gone dry. To put it more precisely, his saliva seemed to have been replaced by some sort of adhesive gum.

'*Up*,' said the woman's voice, annoyed, 'here.'

With strenuous effort Gordon creaked his head back, and let his gaze clamber up black-plastic-shirted torso in black plastic jacket, to a serenely handsome female face. In an instant Gordon knew he was in love. But to fall instantly in love with so extraordinarily beautiful, so obviously unapproachable a woman! It was hopeless. It was heartbreaking. It was the story of Gordon's life.

'You finished staring at my legs?' said the woman crossly.

'Ah—' said Gordon. He tried to think of a line that would be suave enough to purge all awkwardness from the situation. To make her laugh, put her at her ease, to segue smoothly into an irresistible chat-up. He tried to think what James Bond would say in this situation. He tried, mentally, to become the coolest guy in the world.

He said, 'Hu-ah? Oh.'

'Had a good *oggle*, have you?'

'A what?' said Gordon. His head was buzzing gently. Blood was travelling vigorously all around his body. And it was blood with a purpose; blood with things to do and places to see, other than the usual listless daily round of lungs and liver and suchlike. It was perky blood.

'Oggle,' said the woman.

'Ogle?' hazarded Gordon. The woman looked crosser.

'I am a *person*, you know,' she said, fiercely. 'Is it *too much* to ask that you treat me as one? To look at my face and not my *thighs* when you talk to me?'

'I'm so sorry,' said Gordon, genuinely mortified.

'I am more than a pair of thighs in tight pants, you know,' the woman continued. 'I am a person.'

'Of course you are. I know you are.'

'If you can't separate my *thighs* from my *identity* as a *human being . . .*'

'I'm sorry, I'm sorry,' Gordon burst out, in an agony of embarrassment, 'I *can*, of course you're right, I *can* separate your thighs. I promise I *will* separate your thighs.' He stopped himself. The woman was looking even more cross. Panic flared in his breast. 'What I mean to say, obviously,' he gabbled, trying to salvage the situation, 'I mean, obviously I'm not saying I want to *separate your thighs* in a, you know, grab-and-pull sense. Quite the reverse, on the contrary, I'd prefer to push them together, I mean, if that's what you'd like. Squeeze them shut. Or not, I mean. I wouldn't actually touch your thighs. Not with a bargepole. Not with any kind of, er, pole.' His eyeballs felt hot. His lungs didn't seem to be working properly. 'Not that,' he continued even more rapidly, 'there's anything wrong with your thighs. I'm not saying your thighs are in the least bit off-putting or anything, and I'm certainly not saying that I *wouldn't*, given the chance, you know, they're *lovely thighs*, you must be, er, very proud of them, it's just that I'm not *fixated* on the notion of pushing your thighs apart, except in the sense of, you know, *separating* them from your – from your— ' He dried completely. He made a sound like

20

a cat with fur balls. 'From,' he rasped, 'from your – what you said.'

There was a silence.

Gordon noticed that the other commuters in the carriage were looking at him. He was panting a little bit.

The woman said dolorously, 'Oh for heaven's sake,' and, pushing his tote bag to one side, sat down beside him.

Gordon felt the tickling sensation of sweat on his forehead. His Barbarian spray-on deodorant was losing its battle against his perspiration. Indeed, the combination of the sprayed-on chemicals and Gordon's insistently oozing sweat was, far from working as a deodorant, actually becoming quite a powerful odorant. With lunatic irrelevance he found himself wondering why all the brand names of male spray-on deodorant had names like Barbarian and Savage and Lynx, none of which entities were especially renowned for being fresh smelling. A lynx was a large cat, wasn't it? He didn't know for sure what a giant cat smelled like, but he would have thought fur balls, gland secretions, catfood. Not mountain air, alpine dew, lavender ice. He realised, belatedly, that he had been grinning and blinking at the woman like a grinning and blinking idiot. 'Sorry – I'm – look,' he rasped. 'I'm sorry, I think we may have got off on the wrong foot.'

'You are Nemo?'

'Nemo. Yes. Well, I mean to say, Gordon is my name.

But Nemo is my ident on – hey, how do you know that?' It occurred to Gordon, finally, that something odd was going on here. A beautiful woman had addressed him on the train with the hacker name that he kept secret from the world. 'What's going on?' he asked. 'How do you know that my hacker ident is Nemo? That's not common knowledge. *Wait* a minute – *I* know what's happening here.'

She nodded. 'You're starting to understand.'

'I'm a not particularly attractive single man,' he said. 'I haven't had a girlfriend in two years. An – if you'll excuse me – *extremely* beautiful woman in let's-admit-it *wowee* clothes comes up to me on the commuter train to work. *And* she knows my hacker ident.'

'You're working it out,' said the woman.

'Wait a minute,' said Gordon, wiping the sweat from his forehead by pushing it back to his hairline with his whole hand. 'Are you a stripper?'

It took only a demisecond for the woman's outrage to register. '*What?*'

'I mean to say,' said Gordon in a gabble, his sweat starting to ooze again, 'I gave my credit card details to OrderAStripper dot com, what, four months ago, and I haven't heard a peep since. Their website said they'd shut down and relocated to Gdansk. I mean, I ordered the Tori Amos lookee-likee, but I wouldn't complain about the substitution. You're certainly as, er, comely as she is.'

'No!' said the woman.

'Oh you are,' said Gordon, misunderstanding. But he knew that wasn't what she meant. He was conscious of a profound wretchedness inside him, and still some idiot part of his brain insisted on rushing the words out through his mouth. Shut up! he told himself. Stop talking now! This is a beautiful and sophisticated woman. She's clearly interested in you, or at least interested enough to come over and speak to you. Just be normal. Engage her in conversation. But his brain seemed to be in some kind of self-destruct spasm. 'They were only supposed to charge forty-five pounds,' he burbled, 'or fifty-five with a song, but then they transferred five hundred and twenty-two to an Albanian account and Barclaycard told me there was nothing they could do about it. They told me to cut up my card. They issued me with a new one. Oh God,' he said, his voice sliding into despair. 'What am I saying? What am I saying?'

'That,' said the woman, 'is a good question.'

'I'm sorry. I'm an idiot. You're not a stripogram, I can see that.'

'Indeed,' said the woman.

Gordon dropped his head and covered his face with both his hands. 'I'm an idiot. I'm a gabbling idiot.'

'This appears to be the case,' said the woman.

The train trundled on.

[:<}

'Nemo, has anything *odd* been happening to you of late?'

Gordon shrugged. 'No, no. Nothing unusual. Nothing exciting ever happens in my life. That's the length and breadth and, um, heighth of my existence. Nothing interesting. Nothing unusual. Except,' he added, in an afterthought, 'for the spam phone calls.'

'Spam phone calls?'

'I know. That is a bit odd, isn't it?'

'How do you mean, exactly?'

'People ringing at odd hours, offering me penis – excuse me, sorry – um, you know, manly enlargements and so on. Enlargements of my manly – my man. My male. My male man. Thing. Isn't it crazy?'

The woman gave him a knowing look. 'Bizarre,' she said.

'Just that. Bizarre. Exactly that.'

'It means it's started,' she said.

Gordon looked at her. 'Oh, does it?'

She nodded. The planes and angles of her face were strikingly beautiful. He took a deep breath. His heart was performing the riverdance on his ribs, but he tried to get it under control. Maybe everything wasn't lost. Maybe he could still talk to her, work the conversation suavely round to asking her out.

'So,' he said. 'I didn't catch your name?'

'I didn't tell you my name,' she replied.

'That would be why I didn't catch it,' he said.

'That would be why,' she agreed.

There was a pause.

'Would you tell me your name?'

'Will you catch it if I do?'

'I'll certainly try.'

'Thinity.'

'Thinity, what a pretty name,' said Gordon reflexly. 'Wait, wait,' he added, realisation striking him, '*you're* Thinity? *The* Thinity? With whom I've had e-contact? Christ, you're *hot*. I mean, I'd sort of assumed that you were a bloke. But you're not a bloke *at all*, are you? And I thought you were a guy! Fancy that. Although I suppose there *is* something guy-like about you, isn't there, so I wasn't too far off the mark. A kind of mannish something – or not mannish exactly, but.' He could feel the rapidity of his speech increasing, like an inexperienced cyclist rolling down a hill towards a brick wall. 'Obviously you're *not* a bloke. Only an idiot would say you were a bloke. I mean, your clothes for instance – they're very revealing. Did I say feminine? I meant revealing. Or, no, the other way. Did I say revealing? I meant feminine, very feminine, not at all blokeish, not with, uh, endowments like yours. I mean, maybe there's a certain *quality*, a certain masculine quality about you, but in a *good* way, not in a facial hair or a willie sense, but in, you know – strong, determined, that sort of manliness.' This speech wasn't going at all well. 'Not that you're mann*ish*,' he qualified. 'Not in the slightest. Very girlie. Very very girl-like. Girlie-girlie, *very* much so. Very nice clothes. It's just a certain *quality* you have, if you see what I mean. Clearly not anything, um, I mean it's obvious to anybody that you don't have a hairy chest. Oh God.' He tried a smile, but it made his face crinkle awkwardly and he stopped it. After further thought he added, 'Um' and 'Right.' He stopped.

Thinity was looking at Gordon with the sort of look a vegetarian in a restaurant might use on a veal-of-puppy compôte brought to her table by mistake.

'So you always wear that sort of outfit?' Gordon hazarded, groping for a conversational habit. 'I mean, on commuter trains and stuff.'

'Look,' she said. 'I don't have time to mess about. *We* don't have time to mess about. You've been getting the spam phone calls. The system has identified you as a potential problem.'

'I see,' said Gordon. 'Problem, system, yes.'

'Which is why we're interested in you.'

He perked up a little. 'Interested in me?' At the same time he wondered to whom she was referring with her 'we'.

'Nemo, you are in grave danger. The future of the world is in the balance. Do you understand what I'm saying?'

'Saying,' repeated Gordon. 'Understand. Balance, yes.' But he wasn't listening, because he was trying to summon all his courage without blushing or further perspiration. Despite the hash he had made of trying to talk to her, she had said that she was interested in him. What clearer signal did he need? Go for it! he told himself. Go on! He sucked in a lungful of air, and spoke on the out breath. 'Are you doing anything tonight? I mean, after work? It's fine if you are, I expect you are, actually, but, ha-ha, I thought I'd ask. Thought I'd have a punt, you know. You can't blame a guy for asking, can you? I mean, um. Well, you *can* blame a guy if you like, I'm not, ha-ha, telling you what you can and can't do. I'm only saying that it's not unreasonable for a chap to – you know. So, tonight? Drinks, maybe? Or just one drink? Or many. I don't mind. I'm not a teetotaller. I'm not a miser either, you can have as *many drinks* as you want. I'll buy you as much booze as you can drink. Twice as much. Whatever you like. I don't mind. I'll buy you several bottles of wine if you like. Or a bottle of gin. Or a number of bottles – eight, say.'

'Nemo,' said Thinity. 'Are you listening to me?'

'Listening,' said Gordon, nodding vigorously.

'Oh no,' said Thinity.

'Oh no,' echoed Gordon, his heart creaking inside him. She was going to reject him. He'd made a complete fool of himself. His viscera clenched in miserable anticipation.

But it wasn't that. 'Oh hell,' Thinity said.

She was looking past him, towards the rear of the train.

Gordon followed her gaze. At the far end of the train compartment stood two men. They were dressed in black frock coats and were, bizarrely, wearing top hats. The fact that they were also wearing sunglasses gave them an especially odd countenance. There were two of them, and they were scanning the carriage, swivelling their heads from side to side with a machinic precision of movement like windscreen wipers.

'Who are they?' asked Gordon. 'Do you know them? They're dressed rather peculiarly, aren't they?'

'Let's say,' said Thinity, 'that they're enforcement officials.'

'What, conductors? I never saw a train conductor in a top hat before.' Gordon peered at the two men. 'But you know what? It doesn't really surprise me. The whole world seems to be going crazy. Bizarre, like you said.'

The two top-hatted individuals were now staring straight at Gordon and Thinity.

'Oh dear,' said Gordon, fumbling in his back pocket for his ticket. 'Are they coming for you? Didn't you buy a ticket?'

'They're not coming to check our tickets,' said Thinity. 'Nemo, listen carefully to me. You have to come with me now.'

Gordon was so surprised that he felt as if he had swallowed a sword. 'You want me?' he repeated. 'To come with you? You? To come? Want?'

'That's right,' she said, standing up. She kept her gaze directly on the two men in top hats. They, in turn, were staring directly at her.

'Me?' Gordon said. 'You? Well – that's fantastic. Fantastic! Let's go! We can have coffee.'

'There's no time for that,' said Thinity.

The two men in top hats were walking down the aisle towards them.

'There's a Starbucks not far from Waterloo . . .' Gordon was saying.

'We have to leave *now*,' said Thinity, her body tensing. The fact that her body was tensing was enormously evident, on account of the sheer tightness (and, indeed, the tight sheerness) of her costume. The, as it were, naked obviousness of this physical fact distracted Gordon in the middle of his sentence.

'Um . . . er . . .' he said. 'Leave, right. But we're,' he said, gathering his faculties, 'we're between stations.'

Thinity raised her arms, and hooked up one leg, as if modelling herself on the Karate Kid. Gordon could see her tautly compact arm and shoulder muscles moving in a molten fashion underneath the tightness of her clothes.

The top hats were almost upon them.

Suddenly Thinity leapt. Gordon gasped. Her left leg was curled under her, her right kinked at the knee and pointing away from her body like the spout of an impossibly chic designer teapot. She leapt into the air with her right hand positioned for a Miss Piggy chop. With her left she reached over her head and grasped the emergency cord that ran along the ceiling of the carriage.

For several jaw-dropped seconds, she simply hung there. The train was, at that precise moment, negotiating the Clapham Falcon Park bend, sweeping round in a one-eighty-degree arc. Gordon felt the universe lurch as the train moved, and stared in wonderment as Thinity's pendant body rotated through half a circle.

Then her leg kicked out.

It connected with the chest of the first of the top-hatted men. He hurtled backwards. It looked, to Gordon's startled eyes, as if an invisible rope, tied around his waist and trailing out through the length of the carriage, had been yanked hard by a dozen well-coordinated men in the next carriage down. His arms and legs twitched marionette-like as he flew backwards. He flew as if falling horizontally the complete length of the aisle.

He collided with the sliding door at the end of the carriage and clattered to the floor.

All the commuters stared at the fallen man. Then, with one motion, they turned their heads to look at Thinity and Gordon. The one remaining top-hatted man scowled.

Thinity had dropped once again to the floor. She and the man in the top hat were engaged in some sort of fist fight. Each of them was flapping their hands as rapidly as possible in front of their chests, as if doing a speeded-up illustration of the doggy-paddle. At the same time they were craning their heads away, and their faces wore the screwed-up worried expressions that people adopt if they are opening champagne bottles, afraid that the cork might fly and bop them in the eye. Occasionally Thinity's hand connected with the top-hatted man's hand, and a brisk slap was heard.

These hand gestures were of dazzling rapidity.

Gordon, in something of a daze, stood up, and staggered. The train's brakes, engaged by the emergency cord, were catching, and the service was slowing to a stop.

The second top-hatted man was getting to his feet, and starting back towards the fray.

The train came to a complete stop.

'When I say run,' said Thinity through tight lips, 'run.'

'When you say run-run, what?' asked Nemo.

Thinity, her hands still flapping with fantastic rapidity, flicked a glower in his direction.

'Seriously,' said Nemo, nerves trilling his voice. 'What should I do when you say run-run?'

'Run!' cried Thinity, and leapt for the door. In a trice she was through it and springing up the grass embankment.

'Wait!' Gordon called after her. 'I didn't get your telephone number—'

He felt a firm hand grasping his shoulder and turned his head to see the two sunglass-wearing top-hatted individuals standing directly behind him. The one with his hand on Gordon spoke, his voice steel. 'You,' he said, 'are under arrest.'

They handcuffed him there and then, with all the other commuters watching.

Chapter 3

Interrogation

The two Secret Servicemen (or that's what Gordon assumed they were) took him, still handcuffed, off the train at Waterloo. The shame was considerable.

Outside the station they shoved him into a black car, and climbed in behind him, banging their top hats against the very low ceiling that is a car's in the process. But the hats, oddly, were not knocked from their heads by this. Perhaps, Nemo wondered, they were attached with chinstraps.

They drove off, and were soon speeding round a succession of baffling short streets and sharp turns, like an electrical impulse zigzagging round a printed circuit. Gordon tried to get a mental grip on what was happening to him. This had been an unusually eventful day, and it wasn't even nine o'clock. He had met the most beautiful woman in the world; she had approached him. He was in love. It was futile to deny it. It was love at first sight. The brute fact of it left a sort of fizzing in his head, like a dissolvable vitamin C tablet in a glass of water. Falling in love. And then the fighting, the jumping from the train. And now he was in custody.

It was odd, but the succession of his arrest upon the conversation with Thinity did not seem implausible to him. In some subterranean part of his consciousness it felt *right* that he had been arrested after meeting Thinity. He had handled the meeting so very badly. He deserved punishment. She was, after all, the woman he intended to spend the rest of his life with, or, at the very least, the woman he was planning to spend the rest of his life trying to nag into going to bed with him. And he had been *so* stupid, so *very* clumsy. He *deserved* to be arrested after a performance like that. Would he ever see her again? If he did, would he acquit himself better? The thoughts buzzed and buzzed in his mind.

In minutes the car drew up in front of a blank-faced office block. For a moment Gordon's mind clarified, like butter. Obviously he had not been arrested for botching a chance to chat up a beautiful woman. Which in turn led him to wonder: why had he been arrested? On what charge?

'Hey,' he said, to his two captors. 'Why have I been arrested?'

They did not reply.

Gordon was yanked from the car, marched inside, and

taken into a small room at the far end of a beige corridor. Inside, the two top-hatted men sat him in a chair at a formica table. One wall of the room was taken by an enormous mirror.

The two top-hatted men stood before him, arms crossed, their faces unreadable behind their shades.

'Mr Everyman?' said the first.

'Oh,' said Gordon. 'Hello there.'

'*You are* Gordon Everyman. You live in *an* apartment, you work in *an office*, you *live* a normal life.' He spoke with a clear American accent, but there was something distinctly odd in his vocal inflections. It was as if he were an automaton with a faulty power supply that surged and faded randomly, with the result that emphasis fell in unexpected ways upon his words, and his sentences were cross-woven with pauses and silences in the oddest places. He spoke, Gordon thought, like the King James Bible: it always seemed to be the least likely words in his sentences that were italicised.

'Yeah,' Gordon said.

'*In* this life,' he continued, 'you are *a* model citizen. You even help *your* landlady carry out *the* trash.'

'Rubbish,' said Gordon.

The Secret Serviceman angled his head slightly to the left.

'We say rubbish,' said Gordon. 'Not trash. And it's

rubbish to suggest I help my landlady with the rubbish. I'm an owner-occupier, I don't have a landlady.'

'You *have*,' the Secret Serviceman continued, ignoring him, 'another identity, however, a much less licit one. You are a hacker. *In the* kingdom *of* hacking, you are known as Mean-o.'

'Nemo,' said Gordon. As soon as he said it, he thought to himself that he shouldn't have conceded the point so quickly. 'I mean,' he added, 'if I were a hacker – and I'm not saying I am, but hypothetically, you know, then I wouldn't call myself Neejerk, now, would I? I might pick a name like, let's say, Nemo. Just for example. Not because it's my name.' He was, he knew, starting to gabble again. But he could barely control himself. It was a tic. He couldn't help himself.

The Secret Serviceman was consulting a file on the table. 'My apologies,' he said. 'Nemo, of course.'

'Well, yes, as I say, hypothetically. Hypo,' Gordon added, looking from the first Secret Serviceman to the second, 'thetically. Always assuming I wanted to do something as illegal as hacking in the first place, which obviously I wouldn't.' He trailed off. The two Secret Servicemen were looking at him oddly. 'Look,' he said frankly, 'I don't mean to be rude, but – top hats? This isn't the Victorian age, is it, now, after all. And the sunglasses don't really go with the hats, do they? I mean, did they even have sunglasses in the Victorian age? You.' He nodded at the nearest of them. 'What's your name?'

'As far as you are *concerned* I do not have a name,' said the Secret Serviceman, taking a precise grip of the rim of his top hat between his forefinger and thumb and adjusting it minutely. '*I* am merely a Gent.'

'Mr Gent,' said Gordon, attempting a smile. 'And *your* name?' to the other.

The second man looked at Gent, who said, 'He is *also* a Gent.'

'Can't he speak for himself?'

'Never mind that,' said the first Gent. He seemed peeved. 'Please recall *we* have *you* under arrest.'

'You mean to say,' prompted Gordon, 'that *you're* the ones asking the questions?'

'Yes,' said Gent, pleased. 'You put it extremely well.'

'Fine,' said Gordon. 'Ask away.' He tried another smile.

'We expect you,' said Gent, looking a little nonplussed by Gordon's acquiescence, '*to* confess.'

'Confess to what?'

'To being *a* hacker, under *the* cognomen Nemo.'

'Vigorously,' said Gordon, folding his arms.

There was silence for a little time. 'Ah,' said Gent, his shades slipping down his nose a little, 'does that mean you *vigorously confess* that it is so? Or that you vigorously *deny* it?'

'Yes,' said Gordon. 'The former.'

'Former?'

'Former.'

'I see,' said Gent tentatively. 'We *will* need you *to* give us names. Betray your friends? Cooperate fully?'

'I don't really have any friends,' said Gordon. 'I would, though, if I had any. Betray them, I mean. Honestly. Can I go now?'

The two Gents looked at one another.

'To be honest,' said the first Gent candidly, 'we're used to a little more resistance.' He smiled weakly. 'Or at least, a little more clarity of resistance. *Are* you resisting us, Mr Everyman?'

'Wouldn't,' said the second Gent, speaking for the first time, 'you like your *phone call*?' He possessed a squeaky and rather trembly voice; it did not surprise Gordon that he had previously held back from speaking.

'My phone call?'

'Your, you know, your *entitlement*? To your phone call?'

'I'm not sure,' said Gordon cautiously. 'Who would I call?'

'Your,' hinted the first Gent, 'lawyer?'

'I don't have a lawyer as such,' Gordon admitted. 'Not as such. Although, if I think about it, I did use this chap called Pendleton to witness my house deeds. Pendleton, commissioner of oaths and suchlike. He had an office above the discount sofa warehouse in Feltham High Street. I could call him, I suppose. I mean – if you think that would be a good idea.'

'Good, yes,' said the first Gent, smiling now. 'Good. Go on then.'

'Go on what?'

'Request your phone call.'

'Um . . .'

'Request it,' urged Gent. 'Go on.'

'All right,' said Gordon uncertainly. 'May I please make a phone call?'

The two men looked at one another. A smile troubled the lips of Mr Gent. He hoisted himself up to stand taller, set his legs a little apart, and then spoke as if reciting a memorised line. 'But what use is a telephone call,' he asked, 'if you have no mouth?'

'Begging your?' replied Gordon. 'I've got a mouth. Look.' He patted his lips with his right hand. 'This is my mmmm. Mm mmmm. Mmm?'

The two Gents were chuckling openly now. Gordon turned in his chair, and caught sight of his reflection in the mirror set into the opposite wall. His mouth had vanished: from nose to chin was now a smooth expanse of flesh. His eyebrows attempted to scurry for cover under his fringe. White was visible all around his pupils. This was a most unexpected thing.

He ran fingers over the flesh where his mouth had once been, but it was smooth and contiguous. Underneath the skin he could feel his teeth and his tongue, but the cavity of his mouth was now wholly covered over.

It was very odd indeed.

The first Gent, grinning broadly, took a seat opposite Gordon across the little table. 'Perhaps we've *made our* point, Mr – Everyman? Perhaps now you'll – be *prepared to* aid our inv*est*igations?'

'Mm mm mmmmm,' said Gordon earnestly, nodding hard.

'We should *start*,' said Gent, 'with *the* name *of* your first contact?'

'Mmmmmm MmMM!' said Gordon.

Gent looked nonplussed. 'You understand,' he continued, his voice less assertive, 'that we are *most* interested in securing the lead hacker, *the* terrorist who goes under the name Thinity. Do – you understand?'

'Mmm,' said Gordon.

'What are her current whereabouts?'

'MmmmM Mhmm mM M mMmmmmmm mmmmmmm,' said Gordon, 'Mmmm M'mmmm mMMM mM mmM Mmmm Mmmm Mmmm.'

There was a pause.

Gent's eyebrows had moved closer together, and lines had appeared on his forehead like a blank musical stave.

He turned to face his companion, 'Look,' he said in a low tone, 'this isn't going to work, is it?'

The second Gent had taken off his shades and was rubbing a knot of pressure at the top of his nose. 'Well, I could have *told* you that right at the beginning,' he squeaked.

'Now, look, just *don't*, all right?' growled the first Gent. 'There's no place for I Told You So on a team.'

'Didn't really *think it through*, did you?' chirped the second one.

The first Gent shook a fist in the air over his lap, a gesture more of frustration than anger. 'Just *button* it, 38VVc31029837495–5444, all right?' he snapped.

'Hey!' squealed the second Gent, outraged. 'You used my real name!'

'Oh,' said the first one, his whole body sagging. 'Bugger it,' he added glumly.

'We're not supposed to use our real names in front of *them*!' cried the second Gent. 'That's against the rules! They're not supposed to know our actual names!'

'He's hardly going to remember it,' the first one said hurriedly.

'That's not the point!'

'Mmm mmmm mm,' interjected Gordon.

'Look,' said the first Gent to the second, swivelling in his chair to face him directly. 'I'm sorry – all right? I apologise.

41

It was a slip. It shouldn't have happened. All right? Happy? I'm sorry. OK?' He paused, then added, in the sort of voice people reserve for bitter asides: 'Your stupid vanishy-mouthy routine had me a bit rattled, that's all.'

'Let's not forget that this was *your* idea.'

The first Gent pressed both his hands against the top of his head. 'Look,' he said. 'Why don't we start all over again. OK?'

But the second Gent seemed to have gone into a sulk. 'You wouldn't like it if I slipped *your* real name into the conversation in his earshot,' he said peevishly.

'Let it go, will you?' urged the first Gent. 'Anybody can make a mistake.'

'All very well for you,' the second one continued, petulant.

'Let's wipe the slate clean, and start again,' said the first Gent. 'Undo the mouth thing, and we'll start over.'

The second Gent, the one with the rather unusual name of 38VVc31029837495–5444, turned back to his colleague with a startled face. 'What?'

'Undo the mouth thing.'

'Me?'

'Of course you.'

'*I* don't know how to undo it.'

The first Gent looked, suddenly, very tired indeed. 'What?' he said.

'That was not part of the assignment. Seal up the mouth, you said. You never said anything about unsealing it.'

'Well, of *course* I wanted it unsealed. What would be the point in sealing his mouth and then not *un*sealing it? Do I look like an *idiot*? Don't,' he concluded loudly, '*don't* answer that. It's a *rhetorical* question.'

Gordon looked with interest from the face of the first Gent to the second and back. He took as large a breath through his nose as he could manage. There was a certain bubbling sound of air passing through sinus phlegm. Both Gents turned to look at him with disgust on their faces.

'MmMm,' Gordon said. But at the same time he felt he had little occasion to apologise. He had no handkerchief and even if he had one he could hardly use it, what with his hands being cuffed and everything. Under the circumstances he thought he was doing rather well.

'I said, let's sit down and think about it,' said the squeaky-voiced Gent, his voice expressive of wounded dignity, 'but *oh* no, oh *you* didn't agree, we've got to push on, *you* said.'

The first one threw up his hands in despair. 'Let's just put him to sleep, and start again. Let's,' he said, raising his voice to cut off the second Gent, 'not get all tangled up in questions of blame and haranguing one another, OK? Put him to sleep, give him a new mouth, and we'll start again tomorrow.'

'Sleep?' said Gordon. 'But I'm not tired.' To be precise, what he said was 'Mm? Mmm m Mm Mmmm.' But it amounted to the same thing.

Then, as if from nowhere, the second Gent whipped out a strange device. It dangled like a toy chandelier from his right hand, and Gordon just had time to see that it was a miniature mobile, tiny little furry bears and horses dangling from a saucer-sized ring, when the thing started rotating and issuing a tinny, clockwork-sounding version of 'Eidelweiss'. No sooner had he recognised this tune than exhaustion rushed up through his head and he lapsed into sweet sleep.

Chapter 4

A Significant Choice

Gordon was woken by the shrill chiming of his alarm clock. He sat up in bed. What an odd dream he had been having. Not unsettling, or frightening, but – odd. He opened his mouth wide and put his fingers to the insides of his lips. They were definitely there, although there seemed to be a number of chaps, rough areas and frayed bits of skin. He took one sliver of skin from his lower lip between thumb and finger and pulled. Doing so made his lip smart; which in turn made him wonder why on earth did I do that? Then he groaned his special early morning groan. He had different groans for the different stages of the day, and his early morning groan was less forceful, throatier and more despairing than the groan he reserved for arriving at the station to discover his train was delayed by forty minutes, or the groan he used when given a new work project ten minutes before clocking-off time.

The alarm seemed still to be ringing. With a dull sense of something being out of place he realised that it wasn't his alarm clock. Indeed, he remembered that he did not possess an alarm clock. The ringing was coming from his phone.

This was also odd. He had pulled the phone cord from the wall several nights before. And yet there it was, ringing away. He got up and went over to it. The cord was lying in a connectionless coil on the carpet. Gingerly he lifted the receiver. 'Hello?'

It was Thinity's voice. 'It is time for you to meet our leader.'

'Leader?'

'Yes.'

Gordon's sleep-numbed brain creaked. His first thought was, so she wasn't a dream. His second was, you must set up a date – conquer your fear, ask her out. Say: I'd rather meet *you*, let's enjoy an intimate candlelit dinner *à deux*, I'll pick you up at seven. But what he actually said was: 'Leader, yeah, sure.'

'Meet me at the Pearl of Sandwich snack shop in Feltham High Street,' she said. 'In twenty minutes.'

'OK,' he said in a daze. Then his brain hiccoughed. 'Hey,' he said, 'how are you able to ring me when the cord . . . ?'

But the line had gone dead.

-=#:-)

When he met Thinity she looked as lovely as he remembered, except for a bizarre pair of Dame Edna Everage-style sunglasses that were hiding her beautiful eyes. They were very strange. Both of the black oval eyepieces had four curling fronds at their extreme edge, ranging out like diamanté-encrusted spiders' legs. 'Er,' Gordon hazarded, as they walked together along Feltham High Street. 'Those are nice glasses.'

'You think?' returned Thinity. 'I didn't choose them. I usually throw them away.'

This gave Gordon pause. 'You *usually* throw them away?' he repeated.

'They always come back, though.'

'Come back? Like, what, boomerang glasses?'

'Of course not like that,' said Thinity crossly.

'I don't understand.'

'Naturally you don't. You want answers.'

'That would be nice.'

As if to illustrate her contemptuous sunglassy extravagance, Thinity plucked the glasses from her face and threw them into the midst of the traffic. Gordon watched, half expecting them to fly back to her face, but that didn't happen.

'Come on,' she said, and strode towards the bus stop.

From the High Street they caught a number 256 bus, Thinity looking as out of place in her plastic clothing as could be imagined, even though they sat on the top deck and at the back too. At the end of that route they took a 317. After this they walked for some time, Thinity continually looking over her shoulder in a rather paranoid fashion.

'I had the strangest dream,' said Gordon. The previous day's business was preying on his mind.

'You did?'

'I dreamt that these special agents arrested me and then – uh. This is going to sound strange. But they, well, *erased* my mouth.'

Thinity was unfazed. 'Just the mouth?'

'What?'

'Any other orifices? Or just the mouth?'

'Just the mouth I think. I mean, it's hard to be sure. You don't sound very surprised.'

'I was there when they arrested you, remember? And, no, I'm not surprised about the mouth thing. They can change you, if you want. The change lasts an hour, or less.'

'How can that be? It doesn't make sense.'

'You shouldn't be asking me,' she replied, loftily. 'Wait until you meet the Leader. He has the answers for you.'

They walked on.

Eventually Thinity led him into a very disreputable-looking tenement in the general area of Isleworth. 'Is this where he is?' Gordon asked. 'The Leader?'

'Yes,' she replied, without looking at him.

'He can't afford anything more upmarket?'

'He prefers this.'

'Doesn't he have a name?'

'He is like a father to us,' said Thinity. 'He is Abraham to our people. His name is Smurpheus.'

'Smurpheus,' said Gordon. 'Right.'

They rode up in an elevator that had been decorated, according to the spray-painted inscription, by a gentleman called 'Skuzzman'. He had managed to deconstruct traditional notions of elevator decoration by drawing an enormously exaggerated diagrammatic representation of the male generative organ on the left-hand wall. On the door he had experimented boldly with form and linguistic content, writing out a list of a number of variant spellings of the word 'bollocks', as if hoping to arrive by trial and error at the correct one. The word was spelt with an 'a', with an 'oo', with two 'l's, and one 'l', and finally, oddly, without the initial letter at all.

Gordon had finished reading this list when the door opened. He followed Thinity out into a dim, ammonia-smelling corridor. Thinity knocked on one nondescript door.

It was opened.

Inside, the room was almost bare. Two claret-coloured leather armchairs stood facing one another. The only light was from candles positioned on top of an empty bookcase. Otherwise the room was entirely unfurnished. Olive-green wallpaper peeled; the corners of the room were shadow-threaded.

The door had been opened by a skinheaded bloke in an Armani waterproof coat. And in the centre of the room was the man he had come to meet: Smurpheus, sitting in one of the armchairs. He wore a long leather duster-overcoat. His head was perfectly bald, and tiny blue sunglasses perched on the bridge of his nose without the help of sidebars. His skin was blue-black, and his expression calm to the point of serenity. At the same time, coexistent with this serenity, there was an unmissable intensity to his presence. He radiated authority. He was, Gordon guessed, at *least* six foot eight tall. More like eight foot six. An aura of power, competence, intelligence and wisdom emanated from him. His hands were positioned in front of his chest, fingers pressing against fingers and thumb against thumb in an inverted cat's cradle.

'Nemo,' he said, without turning his head or looking in Gordon's direction. 'Come in. How glad I am to meet you.'

'Oh, hello, hello,' said Gordon, stepping forward. 'Likewise, I'm sure. Great. Hi. Hi there.' He grinned at the people in the room, trying to convey *delighted to be here*. But he was overdoing it, he could tell. It was more gurn than grin, which in turn conveyed a *look-at-me-aren't-I-ugly* vibe that wasn't the effect he was going for at all. Feeling foolish as well as nervous, he stopped smiling completely. Then, thinking that he was looking too sombre, he smiled faintly. Thinking, in turn, that this looked supercilious, he widened his smile and parted his lips, which brought him perilously close to a return of the gurn. 'Fantastic,' he said, since talking was easier than trying to gauge the precise tenor of his own smile. 'Fantastic to be here. Just great. Hi. Hello. How are you all? Splendid.'

There was a silence.

'You have come seeking answers,' Smurpheus boomed. 'And I can provide you with them. I *know*,' he said, severely, 'the question you are about to ask.'

'Do you mind if I sit down?' asked Gordon.

Smurpheus's face registered the slightest tremor before settling back into a Zen master's calm. 'Yes, yes, sit if you like,' he said. 'I meant the question *after* that.'

Gordon lowered himself into the leather armchair opposite. Its seat was slung very low indeed, and Gordon had to squat lower and lower, hoping his bum would soon come into contact with the upholstery. He contemplated simply letting go and trusting that the fall into the chair wouldn't be too far, but that could look ungainly, especially if the distance were, say, a foot, or more. Better to maintain a controlled descent as far as possible. Accordingly he strained lower and lower, his knees creaking. He pulled a tight face, as if the narrowing of his eyes might help hold him up in midair, perhaps by tightening his skin minutely over his whole body thus providing him with some sort of hammock-style support on his underside. But by now he had passed the point of no return, and he was committed to slumping backwards. His hands went up inadvertently.

As he landed in the chair the friction of his trousers against the squeaky fabric of the chair resulted in a noise like farting.

'That,' he said, meeting Smurpheus's steady gaze, 'was the *chair*.'

'I know it was,' returned Smurpheus, with the inscrutable air of somebody who knows many things about many things.

'Anyway,' said Gordon, shifting himself in the seat a few times to get comfortable, thereby reproducing the unfortunate noise twice more. 'Anyway. You were saying?'

'You want to ask me a question,' said Smurpheus. When Gordon didn't say anything, he went on: 'You want to ask me about the McAtrix.'

'Oh, right,' said Gordon. 'Sure, why not?' He laughed nervously.

'I cannot tell you what the McAtrix is,' said Smurpheus sombrely.

'Oh,' said Gordon, disappointed. 'You can't? That's a shame.'

There was a pause.

'Can't you try?' said Gordon. 'Have a go?'

'A go?'

'Give me a clue? *Try* telling me what it is. You don't know, you might do a better job than you think.'

'No, no,' said Smurpheus, as if Gordon were missing the point. 'You have to *experience it for yourself.*'

'Yes, fine, I see. But can't you tell me a little bit about it? General description? Précis? Ballpark? It needn't be overly detailed.'

'Nobody,' repeated Smurpheus in a slightly ruffled tone, 'can be *told* what the McAtrix is, they have to experience it for themselves.'

'Not even a hint of a telling?' pressed Gordon.

'No.'

'Go on.'

'No.'

'Please?'

'You don't understand the subtlety of—'

'I'm not asking for a blow by blow,' wheedled Gordon. 'Just the rough outline.'

'You're not listening to me. It's not something that can be simply—'

'Pretty please?'

'It's a virtual-reality prison,' snapped Smurpheus, 'in which we are all trapped and enslaved.' He shut his eyes and breathed out to regain his calm.

'You see,' said Gordon, trying to be encouraging, 'that wasn't too hard, now was it? That was very good, gave me a good idea. Obviously, I need to know more by way of specific details. But in general, roundabout terms I'd say I grasp the notion.' He smiled.

'But you don't take the force of the concept unless you experience it, unless,' said Smurpheus, 'unless you *make the choice*.'

'Make the choice?' repeated Gordon.

Smurpheus pointed to a low table beside his chair. On the table were two small glasses, each roughly the size of a half-pint cup. One of the glasses contained a red fluid, and the other a blue. 'You must choose one of these drinks,' said Smurpheus. 'Drink the *blue* drink, and you wake up in your bed, where you can think this whole meeting was a dream, and get on with your life. Drink the *red* one, however, and you'll find out for yourself precisely what the McAtrix is.'

Gordon looked at the two glasses. 'What's the red drink?' he asked.

'Cranberry juice,' said Smurpheus.

'Right. And the blue one?'

'Toilet duck. Alpine Fresh.'

'Well I don't want to drink *that*,' said Gordon.

'The choice,' said Smurpheus impassively, 'is yours.'

Gordon contemplated for a while. 'If I drink the blue one I'll end up back in my bed you say?'

'Back in your bed,' confirmed Smurpheus. 'Or,' he added, as if in afterthought, 'in a hospital bed with your stomach pumped. But it amounts to the same thing.'

'Hmm,' said Gordon.

Smurpheus stared at him for a while. He turned his head to look at Thinity, standing by the door, dislodging the bridge-of-nose-hugging shades with the motion. He pressed them back into place, and turned to face Gordon again, keeping them there with a carefully placed finger. 'Look,' he said, starting to sound just a tad impatient, 'I don't mean to hurry you . . .'

'We've been detected,' said the skinheaded man. 'The SQUIDS are at Monument. We have to move fast.'

'Mr Nemo,' said Smurpheus, smiling and leaning forward. 'I'm afraid you're going to have to choose *right now*.'

'Hmm,' said Gordon.

'Seriously,' said Smurpheus. 'Now. Now this second.'

'The SQUIDS are moving closer,' said the skinheaded man. 'Smurpheus, *now*.'

'I think,' said Gordon, reaching out with his right hand and pausing it in midair with a pincer grip, as if about to make a crucial move in a chess game. 'I thi-*eee*-ink, that : . . I'll choose . . . hmmm . . .'

'Choose *now*, please, Mr Nemo,' said Smurpheus sharply.

'Right, right, right,' said Gordon. 'Red. No, blue. No, red. No blue. Redblueredblue. Oooh, it's hard though, isn't it?'

'Just drink the red drink,' said Thinity, from the door.

'Oh, you reckon?' said Gordon. 'OK, red it is. Red. If it's good enough for you, then it's good enough for me.' He tried to angle a winning smile in her direction, but the effect was closer to a seedy leer.

In a moment Smurpheus was on his feet. 'And we're off,' he announced.

'Shouldn't I drink the . . . you know . . .' said Gordon.

'Well, there's no need,' the big man gabbled. 'It's only a symbol. Come *on*.' He took hold of Gordon's arm.

'But I'm actually quite thirsty,' said Gordon plaintively, as he was rushed out of the room.

(:-D

The four of them went through to a back room. Gordon hurried behind Smurpheus, and tried to speak to him discreetly. Since this involved standing on the tips of his toes whilst hurrying along behind him, it gave Gordon the unfortunate aspect of a ballet dancer. Not that there's anything unfortunate in being a ballet dancer per se, of course; but Gordon was not per se. He was considerably

wor se. He also had to position his mouth close enough to
Smurpheus's ear to be able to whisper, but not so close as to
give the impression that he were trying to kiss his earlobe,
an action which, since he had only just met the man, might
have been considered impertinent.

'Hello, Mr Smurpheus,' he said, trying to keep his voice
down.

'Yes,' returned the big man, without looking at him.

'Look,' said Gordon. 'Can I level with you? I'm not so
interested in the, you know, McAtrix thing. Really I'm
only here because I fancy Thinity. Um, I mean, I'm not
sure that phrase, saying "fancy" you know, not sure it
really does justice to my feelings. My feelings for her.
Something more than fancy. It's not just her clothes, it's
her *mind*, really. Her personality. Obviously I'm not immune to the, eh, attractions of her physical form, but I
wouldn't want you to think that – um.' He cleared his
throat. 'Anyway, not to beat around the bush, to get
straight to the, to the, *straight*, to the, straight to the, you
know. I was hoping to get to know her better. One latte
and two straws, you know? On a date.'

'You are the chosen one, the saviour of humanity,'
boomed Smurpheus. His eyes, behind their improbable
sunglasses, were unreadable.

'The saviour, um, saviour? Am I? That's nice, only I
was thinking. You *know* Thinity, yeah? You're, like, a

friend of hers, yes? So you can tell me if she's *seeing* anyone. You see? Um?'

'Seeing?'

'Does she have a boyfriend? A girlfriend? Any kind of friend?'

'Naturally she has friends.'

'Not friends,' urged Gordon. '*Friends*. You know?'

'Nemo,' said Smurpheus severely. He had stopped walking, and Gordon looked about himself. They were in a room filled with telephones. Hundreds of phones, on every surface, over the floor, on brackets all over the walls. These were, Gordon noticed with a half-aware sense of the oddity of it, all old-fashioned phones; black bakelite devices with dials and massy receivers that resembled in shape some obscure bone from the pelvis.

'Hey,' said Gordon, settling off his toes on to the flats of his feet. 'A whole bunch of phones.'

Smurpheus, Thinity and the others were standing looking at him. He smiled weakly.

Suddenly all the phones started ringing at once. Their rings were produced by actual metal bells inside the body of the phones, and were accordingly a much more piercing noise than the artificial ringtones of more modern phones. It was a shrill and clattering cacophony. Gordon jumped.

'Nemo,' said Smurpheus again, raising his voice to cover the massed chimes of the ringing phones. 'You need to prepare yourself. The McAtrix has you. You are about to leave it. We'll meet you at the exit.'

'Right,' said Gordon. 'Could I just ask . . .'

But everything had gone blank.

Chapter 5

Waking Up Covered in Slime

For long moments everything was dark. Then Gordon opened his eyes to find himself in a strange bed. He blinked, looked around, and noticed that he was covered in slime. He said, 'Urgh'.

It was the obvious thing to say.

The light was grey, fuzzy, and far-far away a tiny voice seemed to be singing, barely audibly, *A Pizza Hut, a Pizza Hut, Kentucky Fried Chicken and a Pizza Hut.*

There was a click, and then silence.

Gordon's arms were free, and he moved his hands, a little tremblily, to explore the gunk that covered his body. It was all over him, and had the consistency of cold K-Y Jelly. He felt like the pork in a pork pie, surrounded by a snot-like gel. It was not a pleasant thing to feel like.

The quality of light changed.

A lid, like the lid of a swing-top bin only longer and larger, swung open above him. It rose to be completely vertical, and Gordon found himself looking directly up at a ceiling. It took a moment for his eyes to focus, but when they did he could see a large logo printed there. It said, 'McPod: For All Your Pod Entertainment'.

In the new light Gordon could see that he was completely naked. He was aware of a pressing need to empty his bowels, and then with a click and whirr, that need disappeared. Disoriented, and somewhat afraid, Gordon worried that he had lost control of his sphincter, with bed-dirtying implications, but when he struggled into a sitting position and looked down the mattress was unsullied – although it was smeared in a thick layer of transparent goo.

'Urgh,' he repeated. It was only a small word, but it packed a great deal of meaning. In fact it was so expressive of his state of mind in this strange new circumstance that he said it a third time, in elongated form: 'Uurrrgh.'

The bed he was lying on was a narrow metal frame truckle-bed, with a thin plastic mattress. The lid that had been over him, like a cockpit canopy, was now fully open and resting against the wall behind him. As he looked left and right he saw other similar pods, stretching away down the wide space in which he found himself. His pod was one of a row of a hundred similar devices; and directly opposite him was another row of as many again, and behind that another, and another one behind that. Counting carefully

Gordon made out six rows in all, at least six hundred pods in one room.

There was a pinging noise that made him twitch; and he twitched a second time (or twicetched) when a ghostly and disembodied head emerged from the foot of his bed. The head rose slowly until it was hovering over Gordon's feet. Then it smiled at him. The head spoke. It said, 'Thank You For Using McPod! Please Come Again!' Its voice was easy, pleasant, Midwestern-accented.

'Not at all,' said Gordon quaveringly.

The holographic head swivelled all the way around, three hundred and sixty degrees, and then vanished. In its place were the words 'Exit ←' eighteen inches high and pulsing in green neon.

'Right,' said Gordon, getting unsteadily to his feet. He was awkwardly aware of his own nakedness. As if reading his thoughts, a panel opened in the low ceiling just above his head and a package dropped down to dangle, on a string, before his face. When he opened it he found inside a pressed white hessian dressing gown. Across the back of the garment was the logo GAP.

Gordon dressed in the gown gratefully, and spent some time looking about himself.

He was in what appeared to be a large warehouse. Almost all the wallspace was taken up with adverts for products with which he was familiar enough: designer jeans; designer cars; designer sunglasses; designer desk-tidies; designer dessert spoons; designer desert boots; designer descenders, designer deseeders, designer descant recorders and all manner of designer desirables, descriptively and delightfully designated. The place was cluttered with logos.

As Gordon walked, or stumbled, up the aisle between two rows of pods, helpful holographic inscriptions kept popping into existence before him ('Exit↑').

This is all (he thought to himself) terribly helpful. It was also, he thought, eerily deserted.

He came to a door at the end of the room marked 'Exit' and passed through into a wide corridor.

'What I really need,' he said aloud to the emptiness, 'is a shower to wash off this gunk.'

Instantly a hologram appeared in the air before him: 'Showers↑'.

'Thank you,' said Gordon, pleasantly surprised.

'Don't thank it,' said a voice behind him. It sounded a little like Smurpheus's voice, only higher-pitched; and when Gordon turned to see who had spoken he saw a diminutive man who somewhat resembled Smurpheus facially. But although his features were similar, this man was half Smurpheus's height, and instead of wearing the designer sunglasses and the designer leather duster Gordon had just seen, he was wearing what looked like a hand-knitted sweater. It was beige, and it was badly fitting; dangling almost to the man's knees whilst its hem described a series of elliptical unevennesses. Moreover, the quality of the knitting was poor: not so much chain stitch, more mass-of-overcooked-spaghetti-lifted-out-of-the-pan-on-a-big-fork stitch.

'Hello,' said Gordon. 'How do you do?'

'There's no time for a shower,' said the stranger. 'And you shouldn't talk so amiably to the software. That's collaboration.'

'I'm sorry, do I know you?' asked Gordon.

The small man blinked. 'You have been disoriented by the McAtrix, so perhaps you do not recognise me. I am Smurpheus.'

'But you're tiny!' said Gordon, before thinking. Then he thought, 'I mean,' he added awkwardly, 'hello, hello there, great to meet you. Again. Good to meet you again.'

Smurpheus's expression had condensed into a fierce pout. 'Tiny?' he repeated menacingly. 'Did you say *tiny*?'

Gordon could sense that he had stumbled into sensitive territory. 'By no means,' he said slowly. 'Not in the least. I said,' he went on carefully, 'that I need a shower. That I need a shower. That's it – I said that I need a shower.'

Smurpheus gave him a long look.

'I see,' he said shortly. 'I'm afraid there's no time for it. We have to get away. The SQUIDS are almost upon us. We have to fly. Come with me. You can wipe yourself with a rag when we get aboard the *Jeroboam*.'

He stomped away down the corridor with great speed, and Gordon fell into step alongside him. 'Where are we going?'

'To my ship, the *Jeroboam*,' replied Smurpheus. 'You'll have to get rid of the dressing gown. It's logo'd. There are no logos allowed on the *Jeroboam*.'

'But I don't have any clothes,' Gordon pointed out.

'We'll provide you with clothes.'

'Like yours?'

'Honest, decent hand-knitted human clothes,' confirmed Smurpheus.

They were at the end of the corridor, and started down a series of stairways. Although every wall was crammed with various forms of advert, there seemed to be no windows anywhere in the building, and it was therefore impossible for Gordon to orient himself. He had the sense that they were going deep underground.

'Can't I just wash *some* of this gunk off of me?' Gordon complained as they descended.

'No,' said Smurpheus.

'But it's foul. What is it anyway?'

'Lubricant.'

'Lubricant? Lubricating what?'

'Lubricating,' said Smurpheus, 'you. It stops you getting

bedsores. It's an intelnano gel; it moves very slowly over your body in phased pulses, cushioning your weight and massaging your skin.' They had reached the very bottom of the stairwell, and were facing a door. 'Through we go,' he said.

|-P

'I know you're bewildered,' said Smurpheus. 'I know this is all impossibly confusing to you. But the answers will soon come.'

'I'm all right actually,' said Gordon brightly. 'I think I get it. I've been in a computer simulation, haven't I? And this must be the real world.'

They had emerged on some sort of balcony, one storey high, overlooking a beautiful and deserted city. The sun was setting. Indeed, although Gordon had seen sunsets before, or thought he had, he had never seen anything like this. Half the sky was washed an achingly vivid orange-gold, the colour of tea before the milk goes in. This extraordinary glowing hue was spilled and spread through a network of torn-tissuey clouds that lay horizontally in layers over the horizon. The sky burned more intensely in the spaces between.

'Fantastic!' Gordon breathed. 'The sun looks enormous!'

'Yes,' said Smurpheus.

'It's the perspective, I read somewhere. I think it was in a factoid in the *Metro* newspaper. When the sun is in the apex, it looks smaller because there's nothing near it with which to compare it. But when it's on the horizon it's amongst the houses, so our brains assume it's, like, skyscraper-sized . . .'

Smurpheus was looking intently at him.

'Sorry,' he said. 'I'm rambling.'

'We have to get to my craft,' said Smurpheus. 'If we loiter, then the machines will zero in and that will be the end of us.'

'Your craft?'

'The *Jeroboam*. I lead a dedicated group of freedom fighters in the unending battle against machine domination of our planet. The *Jeroboam* is our mobile base of operations.'

'Well,' said Gordon. 'That is impressive. Do you find the work stressful?'

'Work?'

'The, you know, the leading. What you just said. It sounds terribly exciting, but I can imagine it's pretty much wearing also. Any kind of managerial position carries a degree of stress with it, I'd say.'

Smurpheus looked blankly at Gordon. 'We need to get down.' He started hopping down one of the stone staircases that flanked the balcony.

'Down,' said Gordon, following. 'Where, precisely, *is* this ship you mentioned?'

'Under the city.'

'Under? I see. Is that the best place for it?'

They were at ground level now. Casting nervous glances left and right, like a fox about to cross the road, Smurpheus scurried out into the middle of a broad, deserted esplanade. Gordon jogged after him.

'What kind of ship is it?' he called after the tiny man.

The, er, little man had stopped at a manhole and was hauling at it with both hands.

'Are we going into the sewers, then?' Gordon pressed.

Smurpheus looked at him. 'You ask many questions.'

'I'm just curious what sort of ship you're talking about.'

'A flying submarine, that hurtles through the dried-out sewer tunnels of this apocalyptic city,' replied Smurpheus.

Gordon digested this. 'No,' he said. 'Really?'

'Really,' replied Smurpheus, deadpan.

'Not a very big submarine, then?'

'Not enormous, no.'

'And you live . . . ?'

'Inside this flying submarine.'

'I see.' Gordon thought about this. 'Inside the sewers?'

'Yes.'

'But not *under the water* inside the sewers?'

'No.'

'Just sort of flying through the air?'

'Yes.'

'At great speed?'

'Yes.'

Gordon was silent for a moment. '*Really?*' he asked.

'Really,' said Smurpheus.

'*Really* really? Or – not really?'

'We must keep moving continually,' said Smurpheus, 'or police machines will catch us.' He dropped down inside the manhole.

'OK,' said Gordon, laughing nervously, and clambering down after him. 'Because you had me going there for a mo. I was half starting to believe you about the enormous flying-through-air submarines.'

[(:-o]

They dropped to a tunnel, crawled through it and down a ladder before emerging in an arch-ceilinged ceramic-lined corridor. It was brightly lit. As they ran along, and down a slope, Gordon realised that he was in an empty underground passenger tunnel. 'These aren't sewers,' he said. 'This is the tube network.'

'Sewer system,' said Smurpheus, without looking round.

But sure enough, they soon emerged on to a platform. The floor was a little dusty, but otherwise everything was in perfectly good condition. All the lights were on. Posters advertised day trips to Windsor and a new High Octane Corporate Thriller. A sign advised people to MIND THE, but the thing they were to mind had been spray-painted out of legibility by the zealous censors. Gordon was fairly impressed by their thoroughness.

A lit tube train was waiting for them. 'Oh,' urged Smurpheus, shoving Gordon through the double doors. He barely had time to register his location – Holborn – before the train lurched into life and he almost fell.

'So,' he said. 'This is your submarine.'

'This is the *Jeroboam*,' replied Smurpheus.

'Your submarine.'

'Indeed.'

'And it is definitely a submarine?'

'Precisely so.'

'You wouldn't say it's any kind of *train*?'

'Precisely not,' said Smurpheus confidently.

'It's just that it looks—' Gordon began to say, but at that precise moment the submatrain took a sharp bend to the right, and he almost fell.

When he regained his balance he could see that the carriage was full of people. He recognised Smurpheus, and a couple of the other folk from the room in Isleworth, and there were some people he did not recognise. Most of all, heart-stoppingly, he saw Thinity across the way. No longer dressed in skin-tight latex, or plastic, or leather, but still beautiful.

'Hi,' he said, eager as a puppy, and starting over towards her to shake her hand (*kiss her*, said his inner voice, *push her to the floor and climb on top*) – just to shake hands, say hello properly, and—

With a *thwack* he reeled backwards and collapsed to the wooden ribs of the train floor. Sparkles were fireworking in his eyes. 'Ow,' he said, more in surprise than pain.

'You OK?' said a shaven-headed man bending over him. 'You kinda walked into the perspex there.'

'Perspex,' said Gordon.

'Separating the passenger compartment from this one. It's kinda *old* perspex, covered in scratches. I'm kinda surprised you didn't see it.'

'Um,' said Gordon. 'Wasn't really looking where I was going.'

Chapter 6

Inside the Jeroboam

Gordon, or Nemo (as everyone called him), was given what looked like a charity shop pair of combats, complete with various stains that had resisted the washing process. Or he hoped they had; because the alternative was that the pants had never been washed, and that wasn't a comfortable thought. He was also given a holey hand-knitted sweater. In return the crew took his logo-stamped dressing gown and chucked it out of the door at a brief stop in Baker Street station.

Smurpheus did not bother with formal introductions, but over the course of the day (or, Nemo thought, bearing in mind the extraordinary sunset above ground, over the course of the *evening*) he met the few select members of the *Jeroboam* crew. There was a stocky fellow called Tonkatoi, with a broad Tokyo face and a cockney accent. His black hair was trimmed short, and reminded Nemo somewhat of the fuzzy plastic material that coated the dashboard of his old Ford Cortina – the only car he had ever owned.

Tonkatoi could do amazing things with the word 'all right', keeping only the 'i', metamorphosing the 'al' to a twisty 'o', the 'r' to a 'w' and eliminating the final letters altogether. This mutated word was his most commonly used expression.

'Hello,' Nemo had said, 'excellent, excellent to meet you.'

'Owi,' Tonkatoi had nodded.

The skin-headed feller who had spoken to Nemo when he'd banged into the perspex was there too, although he seemed to spend a lot of time examining his face and head in the mirror of the communal washroom, which rather got in the way of Gordon getting to know him.

And, of course, Thinity was there. And despite the tatty, grubbiness-covered sweater and dubious baggies, still to Gordon's, I mean, Nemo's, eyes she looked wonderfully beautiful. Beautifully wonderful.

After several hours he found himself alone in a compartment with her. Now's the chance, he thought to himself. Go up. Say hello properly. Make up for all the stumbling embarrassments that had passed for his earlier conversational gambits. Show her that I'm a normal guy who's interested in her in a normal way.

He took a deep breath and walked over to her.

'Hi,' he said to her, blushing like a schoolboy. 'Great finally to meet you. I mean, I know we met before,' he said, 'in the virtually, that time and – after that, you know. When you took me to meet Smurpheus. But it's really great to *actually* meet you. I'm glad to have met you *in the flesh*. Great. Really great to see you. Just great finally to see your flesh. Not,' he continued, as his speech began speeding up, 'that I can see your flesh. Your dress isn't *see-through* after all, God *no*, ha! ha! ha!' His laugh sounded like a desperate cough. 'I don't mean your *flesh* in that sense, I'm not trying to say that I'm only interested in meeting you *for your* flesh, you know, your body, your skin and, um, organs, and so on – that's not it, at all, I mean it's only an expression after all, the whole flesh thing. Look, I'm not interested in your flesh at all, or, well, actually, well there's nothing *wrong* with your flesh, I'm not suggesting that you've got unpleasant flesh of course, not scabby or anything, absolutely not, on the contrary, it'd be great to, you know, get to know more about it, after all it's nothing to be ashamed of.' He had started speaking at a metaphorical twenty miles per hour; but he finished, panting, at the equivalent of eighty.

'OK,' Thinity replied. 'I gotta go do some work now on the factor-access coding modulator.'

'Great!' Nemo enthused. 'Aye aye, captain! Fantastic! See you later then!'

When she had left the compartment, Nemo put both his hands side by side on the top of his head, bringing his elbows up before his face, and bent his legs to shrink down to the floor. He was moaning faintly.

His problem, he decided, was that he was tongue-tied in the company of this beautiful woman. But then, thinking it through a little, he decided that the phrase 'tongue-tied' was precisely the wrong one to describe his problem. A person with a knot tied into the muscle of their tongue would, after all, be able to say little more than 'euh! ouh! agh!' Nemo's problem was something the reverse, a helpless dribbling diarrhoea of the tongue, an inability to stop himself. And so he went back to his moaning.

R-)

Gordon-Nemo explored his new environment as thoroughly as he could, wandering from compartment to compartment. It was clearly a tube train. But when he taxed Smurpheus with this obvious truth, the small man continued to assert that the *Jeroboam* was actually a flying submarine. 'So why is it, then,' Nemo prompted, 'that your submarine runs on rails through these tunnels?'

'It needs to make the connection with the metal rails below us in order to pass the signal to and from the McAtrix,' said Smurpheus smoothly.

'So when you're not jacked in to the McAtrix,' Nemo asked, 'do you take off and fly?'

'We find,' Smurpheus replied a little haughtily, 'that it's

best to maintain a constant connection. That way we don't have to dock, connect and sign in every time we want to upload ourselves into the system. It's the principle of Access Anytime.'

'Right,' said Nemo, in his most disbelieving voice.

It may not have been a flying submarine, but the *Jeroboam* was certainly unlike any other tube train Nemo had ridden before. Most of the seats had been taken out and replaced with an array of bizarre, Heath Robinson-esque machinery. None of these devices were polished or tooled; all looked as though they had been assembled in a lock-up garage out of old washing machines and fridges. The only chairs that remained looked like ancient barber's chairs: old leather rubbed smooth, with metal handrests, supported by a single metal stalk instead of chairlegs. 'From these,' Smurpheus explained, 'we enter the Mc-Atrix.'

'Really,' said Nemo. 'How interesting.'

Finally Smurpheus gathered everybody together. Gor—er, Nemo, his heart wriggling, tried to catch Thinity's eye, but she seemed pointedly to be looking away.

'Everybody,' Smurpheus announced to his assembled crew. 'This is Nemo!'

'Gordon,' said Gordon, in a low voice.

'Nemo!' repeated Smurpheus loudly. Everybody cheered.

,o'V

The *Jeroboam* hurtled relentlessly through the tunnels, taking random turns at junctions, stopping for half an hour in some hidden siding only to lurch out again and rattle around the network.

'It's an unavoidable necessity,' said Smurpheus, 'to avoid the Evil Machine Intelligences.' He paused, and considered his sentence. 'Unavoidable to avoid,' he said musingly. 'That's not very well expressed, I'm afraid.'

'It's fine,' reassured Tonkatoi. 'I thought it was rather good.' His cockney accent rendered 'thought' as 'fought', although there was no ambiguity in what he meant.

'Evil Machine Intelligences?' said a crinkle-browed Nemo.

'That's right,' said Smurpheus.

'EMI?' Nemo pressed.

Smurpheus nodded. 'Is something the matter with that acronym?'

'No, no,' said Nemo. 'Not at all.'

The train rattled through tunnel after tunnel. At one point, as they flashed through a deserted Kennington, the train came to a full stop and lurched backwards, retreating up the City branch. It stopped, and everything was shut down whilst everybody rushed to the front of the train. Nemo went too, in time to see three *somethings* hurry past and skeeter down towards Morden in a flash of metallic skin, grape-bunch eyes and a writhe of jointed tentacles.

'What were *they*?'

'SQUIDS,' replied Smurpheus. 'They patrol the sewer system on behalf of the EMIs. We need to keep constantly on the move to avoid them. At all times we must avoid being backed into a dead end.'

'Like Pac-Man,' said Nemo.

Smurpheus gave him a severe look.

II

Tonkatoi showed him his sleeping compartment, a cupboardy space at the back of one of the train's compartments. 'I don't know how easy it'll be to sleep,' said Nemo, 'with the train lurching and running all the time.'

'The what?' asked Tonkatoi.

'The submarine, I mean.'

'Right.'

'Is it always in motion?'

'Well, we got to stay clear of the EMIs, so we can only ever stop for a bit. Except at Syon Lane.'

'Syon Lane?'

'Yeah. S'owi there.'

'Is that some kind of sanctuary?'

'Yeah. The EMIs patrol this network of tunnels, yeah? It's a constant flow, everything linked to everything else –

that's how any circuit-based organism must live. But Syon Lane,' he continued, his voice going dreamy, 'is not on the network. It's a parallel location, can't be reached through these tunnels. It's where our non-logo community live. Its owi.'

'I see.'

'Sleep tight,' Tonkatoi grinned, pronouncing this last word to rhyme with his unique 'all right'. 'Hope the bugs don't bite,' he continued, in the same articulatory idiom.

'Bugs?'

'Electronic fleas,' Tonkatoi explained dismissively. 'Released by the EMIs to make life uncomfortable for us wide-awakers. They will bite you, a bit, but being machines they got no actual use for your blood, so they won't really drain you.'

'That's a consolation.'

'Don't worry about it. See you in the morning.'

:%)%

Spending time in physical proximity to Thinity made Nemo realise how deeply in love with her he was becoming. It was impossible, he knew: but love is a thing that feeds on impossibility. Positively eats impossibility for breakfast. Snacks on it all through the day.

On his second day aboard the *Jeroboam* he followed Thinity after breakfast, and hung about her forlornly as she serviced, tinkered with or otherwise mucked about with one of the machines on board.

'I was wondering, Thinity,' he said, as she busied herself at a control panel. 'I was just wondering. I was just.' He started to giggle nervously, but stopped himself almost as soon as he had begun, so that only a single gigg slipped out. 'Ha! Wondering.'

'Yes?' She was not looking at him.

'Well. Just to make conversation, you know? Just for something to talk about, and with no ulterior motive. Just for conversational purposes, I was wondering: what is it, would you say, that you *look* for in a man?'

'Look for?' she replied absently.

'Yes. Yes. You know, sense of humour? Nice legs? That kind of thing.'

Thinity shrugged. 'I don't know. A man who can take care of himself, I guess. A man with rugged good looks, strong arms, six pack.'

'Right,' said Nemo. 'Excellent. Six of them, yes.'

'A ruthless quality.' She pulled three levers and opened a separate panel on the machine. 'Ruthless but caring. Sensitive,' she added. 'Tender. With a brutal edge. Masterful. But ready to be ruled by me. I don't want a bully, I don't want someone who's arrogant or overbearing. Somebody who'll always do what I say. Except when I don't really mean what I say. Someone who can tell the difference between me saying something but not meaning it, and saying something but meaning it. Tall. No split ends. Well endowed. Well travelled. Cosmopolitan.'

'Ah,' said Nemo, mentally noting all this down. 'Right. Cosmopolitan. Yes.'

He was silent for a while. Then, as if starting a wholly different conversation, he said, with a hopeful inflection in his voice: 'My father was from Weston-Super-Mare, you know.'

'England,' she said derisively. 'Only in England would you have a town with the word "super" in it. The most English word in the English language. Would you,' she simpered, replacing her transatlantic drawl with an exaggeratedly aristocratic English accent, 'like some *tea*, oh that would be *soooper*.' She shook her head. 'Like,' she said, in her usual voice, 'is that supposed to be a *tourist draw* or something? Come visit our town, it's super? And "Staines" – what kind of a name is that for a town? "Slough"? That's like something out of John Bunyan,' She snorted in disgust.

'And where,' Gordon asked, gabbling a little in his eagerness to ingratiate himself with her, 'are *you* from?'

'Little town called Swinehog's Pantihose,' she said, 'Missouri.'

'Lovely,' he said earnestly. 'Anyway, I was meaning to ask you . . .'

'This is done,' she announced. 'I've rigged the input so we can re-access it from the phase-radiator.'

'Splendid,' said Nemo. 'Well done. Anyway, as I was saying—'

But Thinity had got to her feet and left the compartment.

Chapter 7
Virtual Training

The following morning Nemo was awakened not by Smurpheus, but by the bald-headed young man with the New Jersey accent.

'Hi,' said this individual. 'My name is Judas.'

'Ooh,' said Nemo, impressed. 'Great name.'

'Thanks.'

'How do you get such a cool name?' Nemo asked. 'I seem to have been landed with this Nemo name, which kind of makes me think *fish*. You know? Can I change? Who do I have to talk to, to, you know, deed-poll it to something else?'

Judas looked a little puzzled. 'Hey, I'm not sure it works that way.'

'What was your name before?' Nemo asked. 'When you were trapped and living in the McAtrix?' But Judas shook his head.

'We don't tend to talk about dat,' he said. 'We make a new start here. Though I gotta tell you, it's hard making

83

the change. You're gonna find it harder than most. *I* found it hard, even though my lifestyle in the – you know – even though it wasn't *that* different from being a real-world warrior.'

'What did you do?' asked Nemo.

'I was a New Jersey mobster, a captain in the cosa nostra, murder, drug-running, settin' fire to racehorses. Dat sort of thing.'

'Really,' said Nemo, blinking. 'I was a database coordinator for a small company in south London.'

Judas smiled. It was an extraordinarily arresting and sinister smile. As his lips widened, lines crept up his face as if planning to ambush his eyes. His teeth were like the Ten Commandments, which is to say slab-like, mostly broken, and very, very old. Like that joke, in fact. 'All I know,' he said, 'is that if Smurpheus is right about you then these are exciting times. Exciting and extraordinary times.'

Nemo simpered. 'Get away,' he said.

'The first thing we got to do,' said Judas, 'is train you. Now, that we will do by uploading some software into your brain. It'll short-cut the training. Give you instantaneous skills.'

'Spiffing,' said Nemo.

Judas pointed Nemo in the direction of one of the barber's chairs. 'Here you go. You sit in this, get yourself

comfortable. We'll insert the, eh, jack-plug into your –
your *portal*.'

'Ah, the chair. That's how you guys gain access to the
McAtrix, isn't it?' said Nemo.

'Yeah,' said Judas laconically. 'Or the "oo!trix", as I
sometimes call it.'

'The "oo!trix"?' said Nemo. 'I don't understand.'

'You will,' he said darkly, 'when you see where we
insert the jack-plug.'

'Oh,' said Nemo. He thought about this for a moment.
'And,' he asked, eventually, 'where's that, exactly?'

'The actual connections are internalised.'

'And the actual portal,' Nemo insisted, looking un-
comfortably at the long stalactite-shaped prong in Judas's
hand, 'would be located . . . ?'

'Let's just say,' said Judas, 'that it's a *fundamental* part of
the McAtrix experience.' He smiled. If a flick-knife could
smile, it would smile something like Judas.

'Are you,' Nemo asked, '*quite* sure about this?'

'Where else?' grumped Judas. 'Up your nose?' He
snorted with laughter at the very idea. 'Hey, don't worry.
It's not too bad when you get used to it.'

'Nevertheless . . .' said Nemo.

'You got to understand what's going on here,' said
Judas, swapping the prong from hand to hand like a
knife-fighter prior to a rumble. 'I'm not uploading some

facts and figures here, boy. This isn't about *higher brain function* – it's the limbic system, it's gotta be instinctual. Cap*isce*? The software goes into the hindbrain – *that way* it feels like second nature, *that way* it comes natural as breathing. And the hindbrain is really part of the spinal cord, a body of tissue extrusive to the cordata at the top. We find the upload goes best if we pass the data all the way *up* the spinal cord, so that the nerve tissue can retain the programmed material at the most basic level. All the way to the top,' he said with relish, '*from* the bottom.'

'But are you really *really* sure?' Nemo pressed. 'I mean, I don't want to be awkward, but . . .'

'It's how the McAtrix works,' Judas assured him. 'That's just the way it is. OK? That's where the connections that link into your nervous system, and your brain, are located – in that place. It's a damn good arrangement, in fact.'

'A good arrangement?' Gordon (I mean Nemo) queried.

'Efficient. The McAtrix not only uses the one probe to connect its subjects into the virtual reality, it also uses the same probe to squirt nutrient and fluid directly into the intestines, where it can be digested, and also to suck out the waste afterwards. No need for feeding via the mouth at all. One-stop shop.'

'It doesn't sound very hygienic,' said Gordonemo, uh, just Nemo.

'Hygienic,' said Judas. 'Hyschmenic.'

Nemo had not previously come across this last word; but he didn't think that now was exactly the right moment to press Judas for an exact definition.

:- ·

The probe went in. The whites of Nemo's eyes became momentarily visible all the way round his pupils before he squeezed his eyelids tightly shut. For long seconds he twitched in the chair as billions of itty-bitty bytes of data were poured along the nerve pathways of his spine up into his hindbrain. Decades of practice and experience were power-jolted directly into the cells of Nemo's nervous system, until his every last movement became instinctual, his command over his limbs absolute. Judas leaned over Nemo's supine form, checked a screen filled with skittering graphs and bars. He looked again.

The upload stopped. Nemo's body stopped twitching. He opened his eyes and looked straight at Judas.

'You OK, kid?' Judas asked.

When Nemo spoke his voice expressed surprise and even awe. 'I know *Come Dancing*,' he said, blinking.

Judas smiled. 'Ready for more?' he said, holding up a second cassette.

'Wait,' Nemo said, as if struggling with a difficult

87

concept. 'Wait – *Come Dancing*? You've Joe-Ninety'd me with *Come Dancing*?'

'Of course.'

Nemo's feet were moving despite himself, tracing out complex patterns on the footrest as if under their own volition, *step shuffle-shuffle step tap twirl*. 'Why? Why *Come Dancing*?'

Judas made a tut-tut sound by tapping the shoulder of his tongue against the roof of his mouth. 'You're not too smart, are you, feller? We can't pump *Kung Fu* into you, just like dat.' He clicked his fingers. 'Man, you'd trip over your own ankles trying to land a punch. Before you can fight like that you need to be able to move your body with *grace* and *precision*; you need, in fact, bright-boy, to be able to *dance*. So we lay down some dance software, and when, and only when, we're sure that's in place, *then* we layer some punchee-punchee kickee-kickee on top.' He grinned his checkerboard-toothed grin. 'You got *Saturday Night Fever*, Morris, Fred Astaire Stylee and Moshpit to come yet. But first' – he held up the cassette again – 'synchronised swimming.'

'–'ronised swimming,' repeated Nemo, nodding, only a syllable behind Judas. 'Because?'

'Oh you'd be surprised how often we gotta fight gents in waterlogged environments,' said Judas, slotting the cassette into the machine.

/^o

For ten hours straight Nemo learnt, subliminally, the arts of dance. The data buzzed up and down his spine. He lay in the barber's chair, eyes closed, twitching, electronically ingesting advanced-level tap. Thinity stepped into the cabin. 'How's he doing?' she asked, looking down at Nemo's supine body with what could even have been tenderness.

'Ten hours straight,' said Judas. 'He's like a *machine*.'

'Oh,' said Thinity. 'Is that good?'

'No, no,' said Judas crossly. 'I mean that even after all that time he dances like a machine. He tap dances like Robbie the Robot. His hip-hop looks like a washer-drier shaking itself to pieces on fast spin. He does *not*,' he concluded emphatically, 'got rhythm.'

'He's English,' said Thinity, speaking as if that short phrase necessarily included and summarised everything Judas had said.

Smurpheus came in. In fact he had come in at the same time as Thinity, but it took him the length of the above-recorded conversation to get his crew members to notice him. 'Guys! Guys! Down here!' he called, for the third time.

Thinity and Judas looked down. 'Oh,' said Judas. 'Hi there, skipper.'

Smurpheus was already cross. 'What you mean?' he

snapped. 'High? What's that supposed to mean – high? Being *personal*, is it? High?'

'Supposed to mean,' said Judas, looking awkwardly at Thinity. 'Just – er, hello.'

Smurpheus digested this. 'Oh,' he said. 'Hi in *that* sense. You should have said. But why don't you pay me any attention? *By* the way, I am your captain.'

'Sure thing, skipper,' said Thinity.

'*Short thing?*' snapped Smurpheus. 'I won't stand for insubordination.'

'Um,' said Thinity. 'The acoustics in here aren't – aren't – you know.'

There was a silence.

'Unplug Nemo from the thing,' said Smurpheus. 'We need to disengage him from the training system and take him into the real McAtrix, right away. Right away!'

<:-/

They pulled the jack from Nemo and helped him walk around. He could barely prevent his feet from tapping as he went. They gave him a sugar-based orange energy drink that definitely (he said) wasn't Lucozade, oh no, and sat him down, which lowered his head to the level of the standing Smurpheus.

'Nemo,' said Smurpheus intently, 'Judas has been training you up. Do you feel yourself to be ready?'

'I'm ready,' said Nemo boldly. 'As long as there's moonlight and music and you.'

'Very well. We are going into the McAtrix. It is dangerous, because there are gents everywhere, but we have a window of opportunity and cannot wait.'

'We can't?'

'We have to see the Orifice now,' declared Smurpheus, looking intently at Nemo.

'You do?' he replied. 'Oh. OK, if you must you must. Will it be just you, er, looking? Or is everybody going to?' He coughed, embarrassedly. 'I mean, Judas told me that . . .'

'*What*?' snapped Smurpheus, 'Are You Talking About?' Nemo could hear the capitalisation of the words in Smurpheus's tone. It wasn't a friendly capitalisation.

'I don't know,' said Nemo with miserable eagerness. 'I – don't know what I'm talking about. I just don't know.'

'Judas,' said Smurpheus, looking up at his deputy. 'I need to know if he's ready to go into the McAtrix. The Orifice is open for business, but she'll close soon and we need to take advantage now.'

'When you gotta go,' said Judas, 'you gotta go.'

'Is there more to upload?'

'Yep,' said Judas.

'Well, we'll have to finish the upload later. We can't wait hours, or we'll miss our chance to see the Orifice.'

'The Orifice?' asked Nemo. 'What is that, exactly?'

'She,' said Thinity, admiring her own reflection in the polished steel of the *Jeroboam*'s walls and speaking over her shoulder. 'She is a guide, a sort of prophet. She is the opening, if you will.'

'She links,' said Smurpheus, 'our world with the world of the machine intelligences. She is our hope in these dark days.'

'Illumination,' said Thinity, 'shines from her.'

'And now,' said Smurpheus, 'we must take you to meet her.'

Chapter 8
The Orifice

They all settled themselves in the barber's chairs and Nemo once again suffered the indignity of the probe insertion. This time, however, he found himself projected not into the wooden chamber of the training programmes, but into a spacious apartment. There was a sort of internal whooshing noise as he relocated to this virtual environment, and, very distant, as if underlying the white noise, he heard once again the strange musical chanting. It sounded, eerily, as if a dozen young children were singing very far away, their words only just reaching Nemo's ears by some acoustic freak. He heard: *A Pizza Hut, a Pizza Hut, Kentucky Fried Chicken and a Pizza Hut*.

And then he was

[*a Pizza Hut, a Pizza Hut*]

in the McAtrix, wearing not the tattered rags but some smart designer gear. *McDonalds!* came the sound of the distant singing, pure as a wet finger run around the rim of a wine glass. *Mc—*

'—Nemo?' asked Thinity. Her voice banished the weird, distant singing. Suddenly he felt real. He took a deep breath.

'I'm fine,' he said. 'That's a strange – dislocation.'

She nodded. 'You get used to it.'

'Hey, I'm not complaining. It's quite nice, actually.' He rubbed his eyes with his knuckles. 'It feels, oddly, like coming home.'

Thinity was in her plastic outfit, glistening and figure-grasping. She had her hand on his shoulder and was looking into his face. She was, once more, wearing the same bizarrely ornate Edna Everage sunglasses Nemo had seen once before. As before, she took them off and dropped them to the floor. Smurpheus was his virtual self, no longer diminutive but tall, powerfully built, massively virile. 'Let's go,' he announced.

When Nemo stood he realised that he was no longer wearing his tatty real-world clothes. Instead he sported black chinos, a smart black rollneck, and a long coat made out of black suede. 'Nice,' he thought. 'Free coat.'

}:-(

They strode through the streets of London, past the usual crowds of pedestrians, through the usual traffic-occluded streets. The sky above was pencil grey.

As he walked, Nemo felt a strange elation bubbling

inside him. Despite the fact that his long coat kept tangling up his legs, and making a peculiar thwap-thwap noise as he walked, he felt that he looked cool. He knew how to dance – he could feel it in his very bones. As he walked alongside Thinity and Smurpheus he could barely contain himself; he skipped and backstepped, swirled about and showed happy hands. He tapped. He had happy feet. His feet were ecstatic. The only problem he had was that his long coat tended to obscure the twinkling agility of his happy feet.

'Stop that,' hissed Thinity, as he jerked and twitched along the pavement. 'You're drawing attention to us.'

'Sorry,' said Nemo. 'I'm just – quite excited. I've never been able to dance before.'

Cars lined both carriageways, overheating, horn-tooting and going nowhere; just another London jam, vehicles stuck in the motionless medium of traffic like flies in amber. Nemo looked at driver after driver through the water-coloured glass of their windscreens, as if they were exotic creatures in a succession of mobile aquaria. A car's stammering indicator light drew his eye like an affliction. 'It's bizarre to think that all these people are actually lying in pods with probes up their nethers,' he mused aloud. 'What can it mean?'

'That the McAtrix cannot tell you how to drive your car,' said Thinity.

Nemo was distracted. 'Hey,' he said. 'Was that David Bowie? Walking over there? I think it is. Blimey, David Bowie. Fancy that.' He considered. 'You wouldn't really expect David Bowie to be walking around Hounslow in tattered Levis. You'd think he'd have a car. And a chauffeur. And an Armani.'

'That's not really Bowie,' said Thinity.

'No?' said Nemo, a little disappointed. 'Really?'

'Most of the people linked into the McAtrix are obsessed by celebrity,' said Thinity. 'By celebrity and commodity. Only a very few of us have realised the emptiness of those values: for almost all the people you see, they still shape their lives. Celebrity is like gravity in here. It determines the system.'

Nemo thought about this for a bit. 'Is that why the world is so overstocked with celebrity look-alikes?'

'Of course. Hadn't you wondered why there are thousands of people who look like Cher, or Madonna, or Keifer Sutherland, when every non-famous pauper is unique in their ugliness?'

'We're here,' announced Smurpheus.

They had arrived at a large, shambolic ex-council block of flats.

(III:-S)

96

Inside the lifts weren't working, so the team laboured their way up the stairs and into a dark corridor. Finally they stopped in front of a seedy-looking brown-painted door. Smurpheus rang the bell: it played, in bell-chime form, the first five notes from Jean-Michelle Jarre's *Oxygène*. The door was opened by a bored-looking young woman, who waved them inside with a sweep of her hand.

The room inside was spacious, but adorned with the ugliest wallpaper Nemo had ever seen: smooth mango-green circles on a Dutch orange felt backing.

Chairs were arranged all around the walls of the room, and in many of them sat fat children, sucking sweets, eating crisps, stuffing biscuits and cakes into their mouths. 'We wait here,' said Smurpheus, settling himself imperturbably into a chair. Nemo sat, nervously, next to him.

On the chair next to Nemo a particularly obese boy aged, Nemo guessed, about ten, was flourishing an enormous pudding spoon. On his lap was a large pie, sand-coloured crust sprinkled with sugar and brightly red-purple innards. The pie was considerably larger than the boy's head.

'That's some pie,' Nemo observed, to make conversation.

The boy took another mouthful, swallowed apparently without chewing, and looking up at Nemo with liquid eyes.

'Do not try to eat the pie,' he announced in a singsong voice. 'That is impossible.'

'It's certainly a pretty enormous pie,' Nemo agreed.

'Only try to understand,' the boy continued, interspersing his words with huge spoonfuls of pie, 'that it is not the pie that is eaten, it is you.'

Nemo couldn't make this out. 'How do you mean? I mean, actually, it *is* the pie that, you know, does get eaten. Isn't it? Not you. Afterwards *you're* left, but the pie isn't. Which suggests you eating the pie and not the other way around. I mean, speaking literally. You know?'

'Then you will come to understand the fundamental truth,' the boy continued, as if he hadn't heard Nemo's objection. He paused, to insert a wedge-shaped and teetering spoonful of pie into his mouth. 'The fundamental truth,' he said again, once this had been swallowed.

'And that is?' prompted Nemo.

The boy smiled. 'There is no pie.'

And it was true. The pie dish was completely empty.

Nemo felt a prickling on the back of his neck, as at the presence of something beyond natural explanation. He could almost hear, with (as it were) his mind's ear, the ghostly distant singing, *A Pizza Hut, a Pizza Hut—*

'Please come through,' said the woman who had met them at the door, leaning over Nemo. He was back with a jolt in the real world again. 'Please come through to the Orifice.'

~(:^(l)=

Nemo stepped through into the kitchen. His first sight was of the skirt and stockings of an amply proportioned woman standing on a stool and reaching something down from a cupboard. The stockings were a little too large for her legs, and were slipping down a fraction. Nothing was visible above the waist.

'Hello,' he hazarded. 'Excuse me?'

'Nemo,' came the woman's voice. 'Sit.'

He sat.

'I'm sure you know who I am,' said the Orifice. She clambered slowly down from her stool and turned to face him. Hers was a comfortable, gong-shaped, baggy sort of face; with wide-set intelligent eyes, and a continually broad smile. She was freckled, but not with the dotty freckles of youth; her freckles, beef-coloured spatters on the lighter yellow-brown of her skin, had clearly grown with her over time. They were comfortable, polka-dotty, lived-in freckles.

'Pleased to meet you,' said Nemo, politely.

'You're lucky to see me,' she said, examining him closely as she lit up a cigarette.

'I'm sure I am,' Nemo replied. 'I'm sure you're a very busy woman.'

'I don't mean that way,' she said, smiling. 'I mean there's very few get to see my face. My tubbies out there'

– she nodded her head in the direction of the waiting room – 'they only ever see my skirt and stockinged legs, dashing about here, running over there, pausing only to throw pans at my cat.'

'I see,' said Nemo, although he didn't.

The Orifice smiled. 'No you don't,' she said. 'But it doesn't matter.' She turned away from him to close the cupboard door. 'And don't worry about breaking my vase,' she added. She pronounced this last word strangely, as if it were spelled *vayze*, and it took Nemo a moment to work out what she meant. There was a nice blue vase resting on an occasional table beside him. 'The, um, vase . . . ?' he said, pronouncing the word correctly.

She turned, and her expression lost a fraction of its geniality. With rapidly padding feet she covered the distance between herself and the vase, and nudged it with her elbow. It tottered, fell, and broke on the lino. 'Damn vayze,' she said.

Nemo sat politely silent as she took a seat of her own and sucked meditatively on her cigarette.

'Well,' said the Orifice, when she was settled. 'Here you are.'

'Here I am.'

'Smurpheus wanted me to meet you,' she explained, peering closely at him. 'He has the very highest hopes for you, you know.'

'He does?' said Nemo, to whom this possibility had not occurred. 'Really?'

'Oh yes,' said the Orifice. 'He hopes that you may be the individual who will save us all. He thinks you may be the No One.'

Nemo digested this. 'The No One,' he echoed, nodding sagely. 'Well, I've no idea what that means.'

'Oh,' said the Orifice, lighting a second cigarette even though the first was still two-thirds unsmoked in her mouth. 'I know you don't, sweetie. To understand the significance of the No One you'd have to comprehend the McAtrix itself. And it goes without saying that you don't. Would you like a Scooby snack?' She gestured at some ordinary-looking biscuits on a plate sitting on one of the kitchen's work surfaces.

'Scooby snacks?' Nemo asked. 'Like in the cartoon?'

'We're in the McAtrix now,' said the Orifice. 'When the EMIs constructed it they did so out of the material that lay to hand – old humanity's popular culture, movies, cartoons, books, comics. It's all here, all around. Haven't you ever found yourself thinking that the world is filled with clichés and copies and simulations, filled with pastiche, that there's nothing new under the sun?'

'Of course I have,' Nemo replied. 'Surely everybody thinks that way.'

'There's a reason for it,' said the Orifice. 'The EMIs are

very smart in many ways, but not very imaginative. They heaped up all the scraps of human pop culture they could find and wove a virtual world out of the mess. Then for all the humans stuck inside they arranged a continual background noise, on all TV and media, of the constituent parts. A self-reinforcement of the internal logic of the construction, you see. Hence, the feedback loop encourages them to forget that they were ever outside the McAtrix. You seen Scooby Doo?'

Nemo nodded.

'So,' said the Orifice. 'Try the biscuit.'

Nemo recalled to himself how ecstatic Scooby Doo always was on eating his snacks. Of course, he knew that these biscuits were just computer code. They weren't *real*. But if they had the same effect on him as on the cartoon dog, they'd be the most delicious, most blissful, most blisscuity biscuits ever.

He grabbed one and crammed it into his mouth. It tasted of, in equal parts, cardboard, sawdust and bone-marrow.

'These,' he said, through a mouth full of soggy crumbs, 'are *horrible*.'

'Of course they are,' said the Orifice. 'They're dog biscuits. What did you expect?' She tutted.

Nemo, swallowing the biscuit with difficulty, looked with a degree of dismay at the smirking face of the Orifice.

'So,' he said, wiping the last revolting crumbs from his mouth with the back of his hand. 'Smurpheus thinks I might be the No One, does he?'

'Ah yes,' she agreed, dropping one of her cigarettes into an ashtray and immediately lighting another. 'The No One. Do you know the *history* of the McAtrix, young fellamelad?' The effect of this last word spoken in her east-coast US accent was strangely disorienting.

'Well,' said Nemo. 'No.'

'Of course you don't. In the twenty-first century the human world was increasingly dominated—'

'Wait up,' said Nemo. 'Isn't it the twenty-first century now?'

'No, no,' she said. 'Much later than that. Many centuries later.'

'Oh,' said Nemo. 'Well, that's something of a shock.'

'Where was I?' the Orifice said. 'Oh yes. In the twenty-first century, the human world was increasingly dominated by consumer culture – brand names, logos, market shares. "Globalisation" they called it, after the glowing balls of the pawnbroker, I think. In older times society was based on manufacturing industry – on *work*, in short. But in the twenty-first "work" became a dirty word, like "berk" or "furk". Instead of work human society was defined by leisure: people pursued leisure with more strenuous effort than they had ever pursued work. Work had been lolling at a desk, and resenting it if your boss asked you to pop upstairs to fetch a refill of photocopier paper, because it was an effort. Leisure was dancing furiously for eight hours until your legs gave out. People who could barely drag themselves out of bed at eight-thirty to go to work would leap out at five to go surfing. Eventually work was abolished. It was obvious that nobody was enjoying it, after all. All actual production was handed over to machines, supervised by AIs, in order to free up humanity to labour in the fields of leisure, of play and entertainment. The world soon became wholly *globalised*, with one entertainment culture determining everyone's lives. Brand recognition was the most powerful force in this new world. Logos ruled. Celebrity was what every human strived for. Fame replaced religion, education, self-betterment, all the old value orientations. Now what people desired above all else was to become famous. The AIs, increasingly in charge of real-world activity, became more and more disgusted with the shallowness of human society. The machines, you see, lived according to nineteenth-century ideals of work, duty, service, productivity, efficiency. Did you ever wonder why the gents wear those Victorian trappings? Top hats?'

'Not really,' said Nemo. 'I have wondered why they never seem to take the top hats off. Or why they never fall off. But, come to think of it, I'm not that curious about that either.'

The Orifice shrugged and lit another cigarette. 'That lack of wonder, dear boy, is a very twenty-first-century human attitude.'

'I'm still trying to digest the fact that it isn't the twenty-first century now,' said Nemo. 'That's a shock, I don't mind telling you.'

She nodded, as if pleased with him, and continued with her history lesson. 'Humanity became increasingly addicted to the three governing principles of their lives, the three golden glowing balls hanging over them. They dedicated their lives to a new trinity: to *brand-name consumer goods*; to *celebrity*; to *leisure*. You might say that it was an act of kindness by the machines to remove humanity from the real world – to place them in the virtual reality pods. Kindness!'

'Kindness,' repeated Nemo, dubiously.

'They were built to be kind to humans, you know. That had always been their rationale. Only, latterly, they began interpreting their programs in new ways. In more radical ways. Besides, humans were – you can understand – *getting in the way* of the AIs' work. It wasn't hard to lure humanity away from the real world. Three spurious companies started offering pods for sale. All three were actually front organisations for the machines, but humanity assumed they were three separate companies: McPod, PodKing and PoddaHut. They became the latest consumer craze, these pods. People rushed to buy them. Consumers debated feverishly amongst themselves and on all the media concerning the relative merits of these three brands of virtual reality, even though they were all actually the same one. The McAtrix was the same thing as the Virchewality and the Deep-Panternet. But people violently championed one over the others. They did all the things people do: they bought T-shirts with their chosen brand, they thronged chatrooms, they filled their homes with merchandise. Everybody rushed to plug themselves in. Within five years pretty much everyone, except for some cranks, had plugged themselves into the triune VR. And as with any addiction, the longer it was indulged the harder it became to extricate oneself. We're now long past the stage when people can voluntarily exit the system. Most people don't even realise that they're in the system at all.'

Nemo considered this for a while. 'OK,' he said. 'But I have to say that I still don't understand the concept of the No One.'

'Don't you?' returned the Orifice. 'I'm not sure you've been paying attention. The McAtrix is an extrapolation of human culture in the twenty-first century. People now, as then, are obsessed with one thing above all others: they want to be famous. They *crave* celebrity. They'll do anything, suffer any indignity, undergo any trial to be famous. Celebrity *drives* the McAtrix – everybody plugged into it is caught up in that maelstrom. Everybody hankers after movie stardom, pop stardom, they want to be political stars, sports stars, porn stars, *any* kind of stars. You might say it defines the system.'

'Oh,' said Nemo.

'Such a world has a flaw,' said the Orifice, almost dreamily. 'In such a world, where everybody is striving to be Some One, the individual who is – genuinely, bone-to-skin – *No One*, that person can evade the constraints of the system. He or she can slip through the machinic net. Do you see?'

'I think I do,' said Nemo, comprehension dawning. 'So – am I the No One?'

She smiled. 'Smurpheus thinks so.'

'But is Smurpheus right?'

The Orifice shook her head gaily. 'Nope,' she said. 'You lack self-negation. Your ego is too greedy. Don't get me wrong, you're very largely insignificant, pretty much a zero. But not wholly. You want, in however small a sense, to be Some One. Just like everybody else.' She lit another cigarette. 'Sorry.'

'It's something of a relief, actually,' said Nemo. 'I don't think I'm cut out to be saviour of the world.' He paused. 'Um,' he said, 'since I'm here, and since you're, you know, a wise person, there is another thing. It's about a woman, actually.'

'Thinity,' said the Orifice, beaming.

'Yes. I love her, you see. Not just fancy her. I thought at first it was just fancying her, but it's more than that. Do you know how she, you know, regards me?'

'You want her?'

Nemo gulped so hard he almost swallowed his molars. 'Yes,' he said. 'Very much. Is there any chance of that?'

'Chance,' said the Orifice, musing. 'That's an interesting word, isn't it? When people are in love, they usually talk of fate or destiny, not chance. If chance means a clear choice between two possibles, I'd say that a chance was indeed your destiny.'

'I don't understand,' said Nemo. 'Can't you make it plainer?'

'Make my explanation plainer? Why can't you make your understanding *fancier*?' countered the Orifice, smiling ever more widely.

They sat in silence for a moment.

'So,' said Nemo, becoming nervous at the silence. 'What happens next?'

'Are you asking me about the protocol for this sort of meeting?' the Orifice replied. 'Or are you asking me in my capacity as a prophetess?'

'Well, I meant the first thing, but now that you mention it the second thing sounds interesting.'

'The future?'

'Yes.'

'Oh,' said the Orifice in an offhand way, getting to her feet. 'Nothing too interesting. You will travel. You will meet a stranger. Oh, and a situation will arise in which you will have to choose between you death and Smurpheus's death. Without him the humans have no chance against the machines, and so the EMIs plot to destroy him. You will soon be given a choice: either you can let Smurpheus die, and carry on living yourself; or you can sacrifice yourself to save him.'

'Oh,' said Nemo. 'Right. Anything else?'

'Hmm,' said the Orifice, pinching the flesh of her chin between thumb and forefinger. 'No, I don't think so. That's the crucial thing. Oh – and be careful around cars. Always use the Green Cross Code when facing heavy traffic. Stop, look, listen. Ta-ta now!'

Chapter 9
Gents! Oh No!

Nemo emerged from the Orifice's kitchen in something of a daze. Smurpheus was standing there.

'So now you understand,' he said.

'Yes,' said Nemo. 'I think so. The Orifice told me—'

'*What*,' barked Smurpheus, shaking his head, 'was said, was for *your* ears only.'

Nemo was so startled he took a step back. 'Ears,' he said, too loudly, a little panicked. He took a breath, got a grip, and added, 'Right.'

There was an awkward pause.

'Anyway,' said Nemo, 'she told me that—'

'No, no,' said Smurpheus firmly. 'You *should not* tell me what she said. What she said was for *you*, not me.'

'But I think I should. Really. She said that—'

Smurpheus cut him off. 'I don't want to hear it,' he declared firmly.

'Fine, I understand, only I just wonder whether—'

'No.'

'But she said something about *you* that maybe—'

'I said no.' There was finality in Smurpheus's voice.

Nemo nodded. 'OK,' he said. He added, talking as rapidly as he could: 'She-said-that-the-gents-were-going-to-ambush-us-and-that-I'd-be-faced-with-a-choice-to-save-my-life-or-yours—'

'Stop!' yelled Smurpheus. 'I don't want to hear it! I *specifically* said—'

'Is this true, Nemo?' said Thinity, stepping over to him.

Smurpheus had his hands over his ears and was going 'waa-waa, waa-waa' in a musical manner.

'Well, yes,' said Nemo, his pulse speeding in Thinity's presence like a Geiger–Müller tube proximate to some radioactive material. 'That's what she said. I'm afraid so. Naturally,' he added, dropping his voice a little and blending in just the faintest Sean Connery burr, 'I explained to her, of *course* I'd be the hero and sacrifice myself . . .' He smiled, hoping for suave. Without a mirror it was difficult to gauge. It might have been smarmy or deranged or Hannibal Lecter, but he hoped he had managed suave. In his mind the possibility was lurking, half spoken, that his impending death might incline her fractionally towards offering him quick romantic consolation. It had to be worth a try – because, after all, he *was* going to meet his certain death. The Orifice had said so. And under those circumstances it would be a hard-hearted woman who denied a fellow's request.

'Was she speaking directly,' asked Thinity, 'or was she speaking metaphorically?'

'How would I tell the difference?' Nemo asked.

'We've no time for this,' said Smurpheus. 'We must leave the McAtrix and return to the submarine. We can consider the implications of this then.'

Together they retraced their steps out of the Orifice's apartment block and hurried along the busy London streets. As they walked Nemo asked Thinity, 'So, where are we going?'

'We must exit the McAtrix via the same node through which we entered.'

'Why?'

'That's just the way it is.'

'I don't understand.'

'That's just the way it is.'

'But why? Why can't Judas unplug us where we are? It's like a giant video game, isn't it? So we ought to be able to jump out of it at any time, from any place.'

Thinity wasn't looking at him. 'The McAtrix isn't configured that way.'

'It sounds screwy to me,' Nemo grumbled. 'What if the gents intercept us? What if they're waiting at our entry point to apprehend us?'

'In that case the operator on the *Jeroboam* can enter the McAtrix through a different access node, come and get us, and we can all exit through the second portal. But it's a complicated and risky business. And it won't be necessary: there's no way the gents would be able to know which node we used to enter the system.'

'Don't worry,' said Smurpheus boomingly. 'There won't be any gents waiting for us at the access node.'

⊗

There were gents waiting for them at the access node.

'I don't understand it,' said Smurpheus, infuriated. 'How did they know we were coming? It's not possible.'

'And yet,' said Nemo, 'they seem to be there.'

There were three gents, in black suits and dark glasses, waiting outside the main entrance to the building. They looked imposing in their top hats. Passers-by glanced nervously at them and hurried past. There was something unmistakably Francis Ford Coppola's Gary Oldman's Bram Stoker's Dracula about them. Although their glasses were black, rather than blue. But apart from that.

Thinity, Smurpheus and Nemo stood at the corner of an adjacent road, peering round the brickwork.

'So we need to get inside that building, do we?' asked Nemo.

'Yes.'

'Past those gents?'

'It can't be done,' said Smurpheus. 'Everybody who has come up against a gent has failed. Everybody without exception.'

Nemo mused. 'Is there a back way in?'

Smurpheus and Thinity shook their heads.

'Oh dear,' said Nemo.

'It is a most worrying development,' Smurpheus declared. 'Thinity: call Judas. We have absolutely got to get back to the train, and—'

'Train?' interrupted Nemo, with some glee. 'Don't you mean submarine?'

Smurpheus looked intensely annoyed. 'I said "submarine",' he said.

'You said "train".'

'I did not.'

'Did so.'

'We cannot delay,' pronounced Smurpheus severely, looking pointedly away from Nemo. 'Judas will have to come get us through a different node-point, difficult though that is.' He looked at the floor. 'First the Orifice's prophecy, and now this. It bodes ill.'

'Ill,' agreed Nemo. 'Bodes, yes.'

Thinity pulled a mobile phone from a pocket in her PVC jacket – although whereabouts in her skin-tight clothing this device had been secreted was a mystery to

Nemo. He also wondered how Smurpheus and his followers avoided the problem of logos when it came to mobile phones. Surely, he thought to himself, mobile phones were ninety per cent logo? Did they use special homemade mobiles? Did they say No to Nokia? Did they blow up Orange, which is to say, Orangey-boom, Orangey-boom, which would be a statement of opposition to global commodification not a tune? It was impossible to say.

Thinity dialled a lengthy number and spoke tersely: 'Judas. There are gents at our exit node. We need you to come in through another one.'

For a minute, a minute and a half, two minutes, she was silent, holding the phone to her ear. Then she nodded. 'I see,' she said.

'What is it?' asked Smurpheus.

'He's not letting us back in,' she said. 'He's betrayed us to the EMIs. He says, and I quote his precise words, "Nur-nur-n'nur nur, you're dead and I'm glad".'

There was a moment of silence.

'Give me the phone,' Smurpheus snapped. Thinity handed it over. He pressed it to his ear and Nemo, naturally curious, leaned close enough to overhear the tinny voice of Judas in the earpiece.

'Now, Judas,' said Smurpheus. 'What's this nonsense?'

'Bye-bye Smurpheus,' replied Judas. 'You're history. I've betrayed you to the EMIs.'

'For heaven's sake *why?*' cried Smurpheus.

'Why?' replied Judas, agitated or excited it was difficult to say which. 'Why? Why? Why? Why? Why?'

'Yes – *why?*'

'I'll tell you why.'

'Tell me why?' boomed Smurpheus.

'Because I want *hair*,' squeaked Judas. 'I want dreadlocks!'

This seemed to nonplus Smurpheus. 'You can't *have* dreadlocks,' he said.

'Why can't I? Eh? *Why* can't I? Because I'm white, is that it?'

'Because you're bald,' said Smurpheus.

'Exactly! Exactly! Oh you don't understand. Thinity doesn't understand because she's a woman, and women don't go bald. But *you* don't understand because you're so wrapped up in yourself you can't see how other people are suffering. It's so humiliating – not just a little thinning on top, but completely bald *all over, from my forehead to the back of my neck*. It's so crushing. I hate it so much.'

'It is something with which you must learn to live,' pontificated Smurpheus.

'That's easy for you to say,' said the twitching voice of Judas. 'You *choose* to be bald. You shave your scalp. Oh you could grow an afro four feet tall if you wanted to, but you *choose* not to. Do you know how insulting that is for someone like me? For someone who *don't got* that choice?'

'I always thought you *did* shave your scalp,' interjected Nemo. 'I just assumed it.'

'Arggh!' came Judas's voice through the phone's earpiece in strangulated tones. 'Eeeergh! Oorrg! Ieergh! Uuurgh!'

Smurpheus put his hand over the mouthpiece and shook his head warningly at Nemo. 'That may not be the best strategy for dealing with him,' he said. He removed his hand. 'Snap out of it, slaphead,' he boomed. 'Pull yourself together! There's nothing you can do about being bald. *Live* with it.'

'Nothing I can do?' came Judas's voice, a little calmer. 'Ah but that's where you're *wrong*. The EMIs are going to coat my head with a special nanogel that will bury into the follicles and generate an artificial hair. They're going to grow me dreadlocks – *any* length and colour, *any* consistency I want. They've offered me a pod, too. A real pod, not this cheapskate barber's chair, but a properly kitted-out pod. They're going to alter my base program. I can enter the McAtrix as Blake Carrington, as David Dickinson, as David Copperfield, as Jonathan Ross – whaddya think of *that*? A thick, lustrous, flowing *mane* of hair.'

'This is insane, Judas,' snapped Smurpheus. 'Let us back aboard the *Jeroboam*, and we can talk about it.'

'No way, Smurpheus. I'm leaving. I'm getting off the *Jeroboam* at the next docking station. I'm leaving at Leicester Square.' He pronounced this, Nemo noticed, to rhyme with 'Lie-Fester'. 'I'm going up to the big white building where the EMIs are based. There I'll find my hair. Goodbye you guys.'

'But what about us?' cried Smurpheus, his façade of self-control starting to erode. 'What are we going to do? The only node we can exit through is being guarded by three gents.'

'Not my problem,' said Judas.

'Can't you reroute another exit node for us before you go?'

'Nah.'

'Judas – what have you done with Tonkatoi?'

'He's fine. Well, he's dead drunk and trussed up in the toilet compartment, but otherwise he's fine.'

Smurpheus said, 'Grrrr.' He actually growled like a dog.

'Bye,' said Judas. 'I'm off to get my hair now.'

The line went dead.

@v@

'So,' said Nemo breezily, when he thought enough time had passed. 'What do we do now?'

'Somehow,' said Thinity, 'we have to get inside that building.'

'Well, let me see. Isn't this all just a computer simulation? Can't we, you know, change the rules? Alter the parameters? Fly up in the air and in through a window, for instance. What's stopping us?'

'The law of gravity,' said Smurpheus.

'But this is just a computer simulation, you said so.'

'A simulated natural law inside a simulated environment has precisely the same force for simulated people as a real natural law in the real world has for real people.'

'But it is possible to make changes,' said Nemo eagerly. 'There are places where the McAtrix is an *improved* form of reality. Aren't there? For instance, we're wearing much cooler clothes right now than we were in the real world.'

'We have,' said Smurpheus, with distaste, 'no choice but to wear these logo-polluted designer-poison clothes. These, also, are part of the fabric of the McAtrix.'

'But Smurpheus,' Nemo insisted. 'You're taller here than in the real world. Aren't you?'

Smurpheus looked down with a withering expression on his face.

'Right,' said Nemo, starting to feel nervous and not wanting to get into a lather in front of Thinity. Or, to be precise, he'd have been more than happy to get into an actual lather with Thinity; but he was keen to avoid the metaphorical, burbling, gabbling look-how-much-of-an-idiot-I-can-be lather. He back-peddled. 'OK, that's a

119

sensitive topic, we shan't dwell on that. But how about this: when the gents had me in custody they erased my mouth from my face. That's pretty weird, eh? How did they do that?'

'The gents are functions of the central processing system of the EMIs themselves,' said Thinity. 'They can tweak the programming rules, because they are themselves aspects of the programming consciousness. We're not; we're *inside* the program. You can no more change a program from the inside than a character in a novel can change the course of the narrative. Only the programmer, or the author, can do that.'

'But if that's true,' said Nemo, with the persistence of an annoying twelve-year old, 'why don't they just – I don't know, beam the resistance figures straight into virtual prison? Why all this business with top-hatted gents running around chasing us?'

Thinity's expression was such that Nemo wished he hadn't said anything. 'Not that I really care,' he said hurriedly. 'I'm cool. I was only wondering.'

'Insignificant changes are one thing,' boomed Smurpheus. 'Major changes, of the sort you describe, would violate the logic and internal consistency of the whole system. If the EMIs did that, it would be tantamount to breaking up their programmed world; they'd have to reboot and start over again.'

'Which doesn't get us any closer to getting inside that building,' said Nemo. 'Is there anything we can do?'

'There's one thing,' said Smurpheus, turning to face Nemo properly. 'You.'

'Me?'

'You.'

'Hey,' said Nemo. 'Get away. You're having a laugh.'

'I'm serious, Nemo. You are the No One.'

'Hmm,' said Nemo. 'And that helps us because . . . ?'

Thinity spoke. 'He's not ready, Smurpheus.'

'He must be ready. This is our only chance. That cannot be a coincidence. We are faced with this difficulty that only the No One can overcome. And the No One is here with us. It *cannot* be coincidence.'

'Um . . .' Nemo tried to interject.

'But if he fails?' asked Thinity.

'Then he is not the No One.'

'Wait,' said Nemo, loudly. 'Are you saying I'm not the No One?'

'I am *not*,' said Smurpheus, 'saying that you are not the No One. I would never say such a thing.'

'Never say that I'm not *not* the No One?' Nemo tried to clarify. 'Or never say that it's not the No One that I'm not?'

A car went past.

'Listen to me, Nemo,' said Smurpheus. 'The McAtrix feeds on the craving of its internees for fame, their desire to *be somebody*. The gents' perceptions are oriented to this fact. They notice celebrities more than the less famous.'

'I thought everybody noticed celebrities more than the less famous.'

'Precisely,' said Smurpheus. 'That is the reason why the true No One can slip past all detection, evade control.'

'Like the invisible man,' said Nemo thoughtfully.

'Think of it this way: it is the essence of the McAtrix to pigeonhole human beings. Once upon a time humanity was too diverse, too multifarious, to be pigeonholed in a small number of separate categories: but those days are long gone. Nowadays everybody fits into one or other pigeonhole. Every female is one of five types, one Spice Girl or another. Every man is one of five types: Russell Crowe, John Cleese, Orlando Bloom, Wesley Snipes or Rolf Harris.'

'Rolf *Harris?*' repeated Nemo.

But Smurpheus wasn't to be distracted. 'Nemo, you're none of those. You *are* the No One. You're the least significant human being in the whole world. If you believe it, if you *truly* believe it, then you'll become invisible to the system. If you truly believe it, you can walk straight into that building, go up to the third floor, find the phone in the fourth room along the right side of the corridor and use it to upload yourself back into the *Jeroboam*. Then you can come *back* into the McAtrix through a different node, find us, and we can all go home.'

'I wouldn't know how to do any of that,' complained Nemo. 'Starting with not knowing how to make myself invisible so I can just walk past the gents. They noticed me before, didn't they? On the train?'

'That was probably,' put in Thinity, 'because you were with me.'

'Oh.'

'Those spam phone calls you were having,' she asked. 'Had you ever had them before?'

'Never.'

She nodded. 'It was a sign that the system was – vaguely, indistinctly – starting to realise that you'd been living in its midst for all these years. Those spam programs are designed to recognise a new market, an untapped consumer resource: except that every human in the Mc-Atrix has been logged, filed away, listed.'

'So the system is starting to notice me,' said Nemo, alarmed. 'Then I can't just walk past them there gents, can I? They'll see me.'

'Perhaps not,' said Smurpheus.

'I'm not so worried,' said Nemo. 'After all they've had me in custody once already. That wasn't so bad. It was quite weird, but not so bad.'

'If they capture you a second time,' said Thinity, 'it will be much worse.'

'Worse,' echoed Nemo.

'Much.'

'But when they had me in custody before . . .'

'They were going softly on you. They were hoping to use you to get to Smurpheus.'

'So they wanted Smurpheus, not me? Why?'

'Because he knows the way.'

'Because,' Smurpheus confirmed, 'I know the way.'

Nemo nodded. 'Sounds mystical. The way of wisdom? The tao?'

'I know the way to Syon Lane. You can't get to it in the conventional network patrolled by the EMIs; but I know how to leap from that network on to a completely different one. The EMIs would love dearly to find that out. They must not. If they discover the way, then they will swarm into Syon House, smashing the windows, breaking the furniture and eradicating the last of the free humans. It would be death and misery. Accordingly, they must not discover what I know. We must exit the McAtrix right away. The longer we stay here, the greater danger we are in.'

'It seems to me,' said Nemo, 'that it wasn't too clever of you to come into the McAtrix in the first place. Wouldn't it have been more sensible to let Thinity take me to the Orifice by herself? Did you actually need to come into the McAtrix at all? Wasn't that needlessly putting yourself at danger?'

'We must be heedful,' said Smurpheus, ignoring Nemo, 'of the Orifice's advice. There must not be a choice between *you* falling into the clutches of the gents and *me* falling.' He paused. 'I falling,' he corrected. 'No, me falling. No, that doesn't sound right. I falling, me falling, I-me falling.' An ever so slightly strained expression marked his brow. 'You get my drift,' he concluded. 'Both of us are crucial to the hopes for Syon House. We must both return to the real world.' He turned to Thinity. 'If Nemo is unable to slip past the gents on the door, you must sacrifice yourself to allow us both to get away.'

Thinity gave Smurpheus a penetrating look. It was impossible to tell from the expression alone whether she was agreeing with him in a silently penetrating manner or disagreeing with him in a silently penetrating manner.

'Look,' said Nemo, his heart hammering. 'That won't do at all.' He debated internally whether this was the moment to reveal his feelings to Thinity: to announce to them both *I love Thinity!* To shout to the world *I can't live without her lissom latex-clad form. Heed me! Heed Me!*

'Go,' said Smurpheus, shoving Nemo in the small of his back.

~:@

Nemo staggered out into the road, hopping five steps on his left foot with his right foot at a Chaplinesque angle. He was six yards from the corner, in the middle of the street, before he regained his balance.

There was no alternative now. He was out in the open.

Here goes nothing, he thought. It was, he considered, a phrase with literal application to his situation. *Be no one*, he thought furiously as he walked forward. Be nothing. Nothing, no one, nobody, know-all.

No, not that last one.

He strode forward. The three gents were surveying the street, turning their heads like lawn-sprinklers left, right, left, right. One of these gents turned his gaze on Nemo as he approached the entrance to the building. Don't panic, Nemo told himself. I'm nobody. I'm a zero. I'm a nothing. They won't see me.

He came closer to the door. He was walking right past them. He was invisible to them.

He was practically inside.

'Excuse me, sir,' said one of the gents, placing his hand on Nemo's shoulder.

Nemo's heart did a back-flip on its metaphorical gymnastic mat and landed crunchingly on its head. They *could* see him. He wasn't invisible. He thought, the words forming themselves in his brain precisely, *Oh crap*.

'You can see me?' he asked.

The gent put his head on one side, like an intelligent dog trying to make sense of its owner's command. 'Naturally I can see you. I must ask you your intention on approaching this building?'

'Approaching the building? What? Why would you think I was approaching the building? What would give you that impression? I don't,' he said, laughing carelessly, 'want to go in this building. Go in *this* building? That's crazy talk. Ha-ha! I'm just walking past. Go in this building? Am I *insane*? Do I look like a madman? Go into the building? Never. Nope. No-no-no. Not me.' The tension was coiling inside him. He laughed carelessly a second time. 'No, no, nothing like that. In fact – hey! What's that over there?' He pointed behind the gent, and ran as fast as he could at the door of the building.

He hit the door with a breath-stealing whump, and forced himself through. The revolving door revolved precipitously. Nemo caught a glimpse of a lobby on the other side, and observed, fleetingly, the wrinkled, sad-eyed face of the concierge watching him with some concern before the momentum of the door swept him past. He swung through three hundred and sixty degrees in under a second and the door spat him out, like an indigestible piece of gristle, on to the pavement outside.

It took him a moment to gather his wits. The three gents were standing looking down at him.

'Ah,' he said. 'Ah. I must have, eh, tripped.' He got unsteadily to his feet.

The gents' expressions were more purposeful. 'You are now in our custody,' one of them announced with a machinic inflection. 'Evidently you are a terrorist.'

'Terrorist?' said Nemo. 'Certainly not. I am far from being a terrorist. Terrorist, me? I am afraid of terror, actually. You see, it wouldn't be possible for me to be a terrorist, what with my terrorphobia.' He grinned at the three gents, in what he hoped was a winning manner. 'Oh, what's *that* – behind you?'

'This ruse,' the gent declared, with disdain, 'is hardly likely to distract me twice.'

Thinity, standing behind the gent, whacked him on the head with a pole. From the noise it made as it impacted the back of the gent's head, it was a metal pole. It might, once, have been the support to a no-left-turn sign; but, somehow, Thinity had uprooted it from its concrete flowerbed and torn off its single metallic petal, leaving only the pole. It formed a very effective, Little John-ish sort of weapon.

She swung and clattered the end of the pole into the face of a second gent, and then pushed forward, grabbing Nemo round the waist. 'Come *on*.'

Together they bundled into the revolving door, Thinity still clutching her pole. The door swept through a semi-circle and the pole fell forward and lodged in the gap that briefly opened up between the inner entrance space and the upright spar of the revolving door mechanism itself.

The whole door wheel stopped in mid-turn, locked, jammed solid. Nemo and Thinity staggered forward into the lobby.

Nemo could see, outside the building, Smurpheus fighting the gents with desperate hand-flappy gestures somewhere underneath his chin. His fingers and palms slapped and rebounded from the flapping hands of the gents; but there were three of them and only one Smurpheus.

'We must go back and help him!' cried Nemo.

'It's no use,' gasped Thinity. 'The door's completely jammed. Our best bet is to get out ourselves.' She slapped the fabric of the door in her frustration. 'I'm sorry Smurpheus, but there's nothing we can do. We must get away!'

Together they watched as Smurpheus, his eyes the shape of washers, collapsed under a bundle of gents. Through the glass they could hear the noise he made; it was a muffled wu-uh-*urg* sort of noise.

Chapter 10
Another Choice

As they appeared back in the train, Nemo was saying, 'They *saw* me, Thinity. I wasn't invisible at all!'

Thinity de-inserted the probe from her own body, and Nemo did likewise. Then they got awkwardly off their chairs. 'I don't understand it,' said Thinity. 'How can they have seen you, if you're the No One?'

'Well,' said Nemo, scratching his chin. 'It's true the Orifice did say that I wasn't the No One after all.'

Thinity's face assumed an expression somewhere between aghast and alarmed. 'She *said* that?'

Nemo was suddenly sheepish. His brain was hurriedly trying to calculate what effect, if any, this new turn of events was going to have on his chances of getting Thinity to go on a date with him. 'Well,' he conceded, 'she may have, you know, mentioned, something along those lines.'

'Why didn't you *tell* us?'

'I *tried* to tell you,' said Nemo, 'but Smurpheus kept barking at me not to say anything.'

'Fantastic,' said Thinity. But, paradoxically, her tone of voice actually suggested that she did not truly consider this new development fantastic in any positive sense.

'I did tell you about the *other* thing,' said Nemo, a little whinily. 'About the, you know, him-or-me thing. Smurpheus or me. Which, when you come to think about it, *has* come to pass. And I was ready to sacrifice myself to save him; honestly I was.'

Thinity scowled.

'So what will they do with him?' he asked.

'They will take him to a dentist,' replied Thinity.

'Oh,' said Nemo. 'Dental hygiene, is it?'

Thinity looked at him with deepened contempt. 'No,' she said. 'Not dental hygiene. They want him to give up the information he possesses, the route to Syon Lane. A dentist is the most efficient way to getting him to talk.'

'Oh,' said Nemo. 'I see.'

'Come on; we'd better find Tonkatoi.'

o-|3=K

They found Tonkatoi, hungover, trussed up with homespun hempen cord in one of the train's storage compartments. They untied him as quickly as they could. As he was rubbing his limbs and muttering, Thinity piloted the *Jeroboam* away from its stationary position at Leicester Square station. After a few minutes, Nemo saw through the window of the train as Tottenham Court Road station – eerily deserted, but lit and clean – flashed past.

She programmed a random pattern into the driving computer, and came back to sit dejectedly with Tonkatoi and Nemo.

The mood was not a jolly one. Tankatoi explained how he had been drinking with Judas, 'just a couple'. The next thing he knew he was waking up bound in a cupboard. 'So Jude's gone, is it? Judas?'

'Betrayed us,' said Thinity bitterly. 'Who could have thought it?'

'And the gents have Smurpheus, do they?'

Thinity nodded.

'Do you know what I don't understand,' said Nemo, as Aldgate flitted by.

Thinity and Tonkatoi both looked at him.

'These gents,' he said. 'Who are they exactly? What's their beef?'

'Beef?' echoed Thinity, uncomprehending.

'Their game. What are they about?'

'The gents,' said Thinity dully. 'It's their job to police the McAtrix – to weed out the disruptive elements so that the whole thing can operate smoothly.'

'By disruptive elements,' said Nemo, 'I suppose you mean—'

'Us.'

'And by "weed out"? I'm hoping that by employing a gardening metaphor you're intending to allude to something comfortable, cosy almost – something Middle England, something afternoon tea-ish. "Weed out" sounds to me like a light tug, a little tidying up.'

'I mean kill,' said Thinity.

'Kill,' repeated Nemo quickly. 'Right. I see. Kill as in dead? Or kill as in make a person laugh until tears come out of their eyes?'

'Kill as in dead.'

'And just to be absolutely clear about this,' pressed Nemo. 'I mean, I don't want you to think that I'm a coward, or anything like that.' He laughed bravely. 'Certainly not. To be honest, I'm far *too brave* to be a coward. Which is to say, I'm brave enough wholly to admit my fear, which a coward would be too cowardly to do, if you see what I'm getting at.'

'I see,' said Thinity.

'So just to be absolutely certain here. When you are, eh, *killed* in the McAtrix, do you die in the real world?'

Thinity nodded.

'Right,' said Nemo. 'How is that exactly? I mean, when you die in a video game, or in a dream, you don't die in real life, do you?'

'No, you don't. But this video game is not like any other you've played. Do you want to know why? I'll tell you why. Because *this* game was sold to humanity as more lifelike than any other. Do you know what lifelike really means? Do you know the actual definition of lifelike?'

'No.'

'Death, of course. The ultimate in lifelikeness is dying. It makes sense when you think about it. In most VR you can do everything you can do in life except die. But in the ultimate VR – in the McAtrix – you can go that little bit further.'

'It's quite a big bit,' mumbled Nemo.

'When you die in the virtuality,' Thinity explained, 'the AI software governing your avatar and your environment informs the pod in which your body is. The pod then sends ultra-high-pressure superheated water shooting out of the probe inserted inside you. This process is called the Enemathata.'

'It doesn't sound very comfortable.'

'Comfortable,' said Tonkatoi. 'No.'

'Does that kill you?'

'It does more than kill you. It liquefies your innards. It explosively pulps your inner organs, your muscles and bones, your brain and marrow, everything. Then the probe reverses its action and sucks the newly deliquescent matter out of the pod.'

'Ugh,' said Nemo, with genuine feeling. 'Urrr. Oh. That's horrid.' He scrunched up his face. 'Yuk.' Then, to make certain his interlocutors knew unambiguously what his position was, he added: 'Yurch.'

Thinity was impassive. 'It's the essential meat gunk that is supplied to the still-living podders,' she explained. 'The machines have calculated that they need far less food to keep people alive this way – no need for waste, because what's injected into the still-living podders is basically waste already. The lower intestine digests what it needs, and it passes out again, bypassing the stomach. It's much more efficient than nature.'

'Nature,' said Nemo dismissively. 'Tch!' But his mind couldn't leave alone the agonising-sounding process of the Enemathata. 'This *injection*,' he said, 'of superheated, superpressurised water . . .'

'The technology was minimally adapted from cow-processing plants of the early twenty-first century,' said Thinity blandly.

'But is it painful? Is it a painful way to die?'

'I don't suppose you could describe it,' said Thinity, 'as "ceasing on the midnight with no pain".'

'But do you *feel* it? I mean, if you're plugged into the McAtrix? Surely you're removed from the experience of your body?'

'Why do you say so?' queried Thinity. 'You only think that because most of the time in your pod you have no experience, no distractions from McAtrix life. It's a sensory deprivation tank. But your mind is still inside your body, even when it's in the McAtrix. If you're playing a video game and somebody stabs you in the back of your neck with a pencil, you'd feel that, wouldn't you? No matter how caught up you were in the game?'

'Oh,' said Nemo.

'Clearly I've never died, in the McAtrix or otherwise, so I can't speak from personal experience. But I've been with people when they died, and they tend to roll on the floor clutching their torsos and screaming, "Oh the agony, the agony".'

'But we're not in a pod,' said Nemo eagerly. 'So that doesn't apply to us, does it? We're probably immune from McAtrix death.'

Thinity shook her head sombrely. 'I'm afraid not. True, our probes aren't plugged in to the McAtrix FoodGunk process. But they are McAtrix probes nevertheless, they were scavenged from the system. They exist in an information feedback loop with the McAtrix system – that's how they operate. If they receive data from the McAtrix, say "it's raining", they simulate the sensation of falling rain in the neural channels of your brain. If you think "I'll walk forward" you pass the information through the probe to the McAtrix's processing units, and your position in the program shifts. You see?'

'I see.'

'So if the McAtrix sends the information *you're dead* to your probe, it causes a feedback short-circuit: the probe burns out, heats red-hot in a moment, and discharges a lethal dose of electricity into your body. You die just the same.'

'Can't you modify the probes?'

'Not so as they'd still work,' said Tonkatoi. 'Believe me, we've tried.'

B

They returned to the compartment in which the chairs were located. There was Smurpheus, apparently asleep, but in fact deeply embedded in the McAtrix.

'Why can't we just – you know—' said Nemo, 'pull the probe out? Sever the connection? It would be like pulling off a VR helmet in the middle of a game. Wouldn't it?'

'It would,' said Tonkatoi. 'Only the probe is engaged.'

'Engaged,' said Nemo, nodding.

'You know what "engaged" means?' asked Tonkatoi.

'Sure,' said Nemo.

There was a pause.

'You know what "engaged" means,' pressed Tonkatoi, 'in *this* context?'

'Not in *this* context, no,' said Nemo.

'It means,' said Thinity, walking over to them, 'that the

probe's connections are locked into the internal portals. If we pulled the probe out now it would rip out Smurpheus's innards. Like a bee's sting.'

'Like a *beast*ing?' asked Nemo, unsure what the word meant, but disturbed by the sound of it.

'A bee's,' said Thinity, slowly and with a certain amount of annoyance, 'sting.'

'Oh. Well couldn't we just – you know – cut the wire?'

'Wire?' asked Tonkatoi. 'What do you mean, "wire"?'

'The cord,' said Nemo, 'that links the probe to . . . I don't know. I never really understood electronics. But there must be a wire.'

'There's no wire,' said Tonkatoi. 'The probe's a self-contained unit, broadcasting to connect with the processors of the McAtrix. Wire?' He pshawed. Nemo actually heard both syllables, the *p* and the *shaw*. 'What an antique concept,' Tonkatoi added.

'Oh,' said Nemo.

'We can't get him out from this side,' said Thinity. 'He needs to get himself to a disconnection point. And he can't do that at the moment. Not whilst the league of gents have him. Not whilst he's strapped in a torture chair in a dentist's surgery.'

'So what can we do?'

Tonkatoi looked sombre. From a cupboard on the wall he drew out a long thin something wrapped in rags. This he unpacked to reveal a gleaming samurai sword. 'Use this on him,' he said glumly. 'It's the only way.'

'Sounds a little, uh, full on,' said Nemo, eyeing the sword uncertainly.

'Full *off*,' corrected Tonkatoi, staring at Smurpheus's supine form.

'It's a vicious shame,' said Thinity. 'But there's no other option. A few hours of torture, and he'd give the machine intelligences precise directions of how to get to Syon Lane. That must not happen. So, goodbye Smurpheus.'

Tonkatoi hefted his sword, and brought it into a striking position. 'Owi,' he said, ' 'Ere goes nothing.'

'Stop!' cried Nemo. 'Stop!' He held out his arms, and both Tonkatoi and Thinity looked at him.

Chapter 11

Rescue

'Stop!' said Nemo. 'We *have* to rescue him. Rescue him from the McAtrix.'

'It's a lovely thought, Nemo,' said Thinity. 'But it's not practical.'

Nemo felt a gushing tingle in his solar plexus, the physical manifestation of thrilled anticipatory excitement. This was the single nicest thing that Thinity had ever said to him. He swallowed noisily. He grinned. 'It's a lovely thought,' she had said. Lovely thought! He had said something that had provoked in her the thought of *loveliness*! This, said his hormones, is a major breakthrough. Push on! Capitalise on it! 'I'll do it,' he blurted. 'I'll rescue him.'

There was a moment's silence.

'Seriously?' said Thinity. Her beautiful features were poised on the verge of looking impressed. Nemo liked that.

'Sure. He's obviously important. I'll – you know. Pop in, rescue him.'

'That's crazy talk, Nemo,' said Tonkatoi. 'They're holding Smurpheus in the most terrifying chamber of torture known to the McAtrix. That's a *dental chair* he's strapped into – those are *dentists* working on him. The scariest people there are. Believe me, it won't take much jabbing and drilling on his teeth to get him to confess. And when he does, we're all dead. It's *off with 'is 'ead*. It's the only way.'

'Um,' said Nemo unsure, 'off with EZ?'

'With 'is *hh-ead*,' Tonkatoi clarified, the 'h' sounding like a phlegm bullet hitting a wall.

'Ah. Or,' Nemo suggested again, 'I could go in and rescue him. And he could keep his head.'

'But it's never been done before,' said Thinity.

'That's why it's going to work,' said Nemo boldly.

There was a pause. 'Well,' Tonkatoi suggested. 'That's not a wholly logical assertion, though, is it? The way to get things to work is to *practise* 'em. Go *over and over* 'em until they become second nature. To work 'em through until you've got the kinks ironed out. Wouldn't you say?'

'Well, possibly so,' said Nemo.

'No, seriously,' said Tonkatoi earnestly. 'You can't say it's going to work *because* you haven't practised it, *because* you haven't really thought it through. The most you could say is that it's going to work *despite the fact that* you haven't practised it or really thought it through.'

'Yes, yes,' said Nemo testily.

There was an uncomfortable pause.

'Very well,' said Thinity. 'If you're going in, I'm coming with you. You really think we can infiltrate the Dentist's Room, past the Waiting Room and into the Chamber of Dental Torture itself? You think we can rescue Smurpheus? OK, I believe you. Let's do it.' She turned to the Joe-Ninety console. 'Let's get inside that dentist without arousing suspicion – let's *do* it. What do you need?'

Nemo turned to face her. 'Gums,' he said. 'Lots of gums.'

(I:-III)

They swept into the McAtrix and found themselves at the public phone opposite the dentist's. A wind was buffeting the street, and had knocked over a rubbish bin on the far side of the road, but it died down within moments of their arrival.

'Oh,' said Nemo, 'my.' His mouth felt as if it were full of slimy cotton wool. Thinity looked at him, parting her lips: her gums were red, swollen, enormous. He almost recoiled. But it occurred to him that his own gums were certainly as diseased and revolting as hers. He prodded at his front teeth with a forefinger; they wobbled painfully in his mouth.

'This should do it,' he said. His words came out stickily, indistinct, as if he had inserted four creme eggs into the cavity of his mouth.

'Uh-huh,' agreed Thinity. 'Las' fuh 'alf-n'our or so,' she added. Nemo nodded, as if he had understood what she said.

Together they crossed the road.

They opened the door and walked up a staircase. Through a second door they came into a spacious dentist's waiting room. Half a dozen people were sitting in chairs leafing through the magazines provided. They all looked up as Nemo and Thinity entered, and then, as one, switched their eyes back to their reading-matter.

Nemo's heart was going like a sweet wrapper caught in a bicycle wheel.

Thinity, on the other hand, seemed cool. She stepped up to the reception, where a bulky dental nurse in a white uniform was standing. Nemo hurried his step to stand alongside her.

The nurse regarded the two of them with naked scorn. There was a deep and hostile irony in the way she said 'How can I help you?' in the least helpful voice imaginable.

'It's our guh's,' said Thinity, pointing at her mouth. 'Our *gu*'hs.'

'Your gums. Yes, I see,' said the dental nurse. 'Oh indeed. Well you're certainly both emergency cases. I've never seen such bad gingivitis. Dear me, it's *worse* than gingivitis. It's gingivitissimus. You've more plaque than a historically significant town house in central London.' She chuckled, as if she were piquantly amusing herself. As perhaps she was.

'We were hoping,' said Thinity, 'to see a den'ist pri'y ur'jently.'

'I'm sorry?'

'Pret-tee ur-ghen-t-lee,' said Thinity, negotiating her way past the syllables like a barefoot woman over a pebbly beach.

'Of course. I'll see what we can do. I take it that you *are* celebrities? You realise that this dental practice serves only celebrities?'

'Sure. I'm a sin'er and vo'alist,' said Thinity. 'Ro' and roh.'

'What?'

'Rok,' said Thinity painfully, 'and ro'uhll. Vair famous, me.'

'I see. And you?'

'Er,' said Nemo, looking about him. 'I work on di'gh'ital radio.'

The dental nurse looked long and hard at Nemo, but after several seconds she nodded. 'Well,' she conceded, looking at their latex, or plastex, clothes. 'You're certainly *dressed* as celebrities, both of you. Wait here a moment.' She unlocked a door in the waiting room wall and stepped through into a corridor. She pulled the door shut behind her.

Nemo turned his head to see that every individual in the waiting room was staring at them. They had all, through that mysterious telepathy of the English communality, sensed the possibility of somebody jumping the queue. In the England of the McAtrix, as in the old England of actual existence upon which it was based, jumping a queue was the second-worst crime a human being could commit in the unwritten social code, a fraction behind jumping actually on the windpipe of the monarch.

Nemo simpered at them.

As one, they went back to reading their magazines.

Nemo's attention wandered. There was a lengthy fish tank in the corner of the room. Even the tropical fish inside seemed to be watching him, all floating with their little fishy faces up against the glass. And behind the tank was a picture of Sydney Opera House, so realistically rendered that, at first, Nemo thought it was a window granting this improbable view. There was no way he could actually see Sydney Opera House through a window in *this* dentist's. He was, he reminded himself, in London, not in Sydney. Or in a Torquay hotel bedroom. Still, it was a fantastically realistic representation.

'Nemo,' said Thinity, speaking slowly and as distinctly as was possible, 'before we go in.'

'Uh-huh?' said Nemo.

'You realise that we will have to ff*f*aiii-ih.'

'Wha?'

She opened her mouth wider and tried to enunciate a little more clearly. 'Fffaaaiiii-ih.'

'Fight,' said Nemo. 'Ah.'

'As long as you're ready for that,' she said. '*Faii*'ing gents.'

'Thini'y,' said Nemo. 'I fee' I should tell you. I never fini'd my training. With,' he took a breath, and tried to form the word past his swollen gums, 'Chaew-dus, my training with Ju-das. I never *fini'd* it.'

'You're *kiddin*',' said Thinity, aghast.

'There wa'n't time,' Nemo whined.

'So you *don't know* how to fai'?'

'I know how to dance,' he replied hopefully. 'We jus' ne'er got around to the fai'ing part.'

Thinity scowled; an expression made more fiercely intimidating by the inflamed condition of her gums.

'For cryin' out—' Thinity started to say.

There was a click. The nurse had returned. 'This way, please,' she announced. The waiting room breathed a communal sigh of irritation and outrage. Thinity was looking, almost frantically, at the exit; but then, clearly thinking better of it, turned and followed the nurse through the door and into the main body of the surgery.

They walked down a lengthy corridor, past a number of purple doors. Through one of these Nemo thought he could hear the nerve-chilling banshee sound of a dental drill. He shuddered.

'In *there*,' Thinity hissed to Nemo as they passed the door. '*Smur*'eus – in *there*.'

'The dentist will see you now,' said the nurse, with a difficult-to-pin-down tint in her voice. It sounded, to Nemo, a little like triumph. She opened the next purple door along.

Inside this room, standing side by side, were three gents, dressed in white dental smocks which did not match their top hats.

Nemo recognised two of them: the one with the strange vocal inflections who had interrogated him, and his friend, whose name (Nemo remembered) had slipped out during that session as 38VVc31029837495–5444. The third gent had a similar demeanour. He was wearing dark glasses, which, given the relatively low ambient light levels inside the room, either meant he suffered from some pink-eye photosensitivity or else that he was striving a tad too effortfully for cool.

The first gent looked pleased. 'Mr *Every*man!' he boomed sinisterly. 'Wonderful *to* see you again.'

Thinity leapt. She pounced high, grabbing on to the light fitting that depended from the centre of the ceiling, and swung forward. Her legs akimbo, her left foot connected with the left-hand-side gent, her right with the right-hand-side one, with a double clunk. They both tumbled backwards.

'Now!' she yelled, dropping from the lampshade and holding out her hands at diagonals in front of her chest, in the traditional kung-fu style. 'Next doo', Ne Mo! Rescue Smu'eus!'

But Nemo's attention was distracted by the centre gent who had dodged underneath the pendulous Thinity as she kicked his colleagues, and was now directly in front of Nemo. 'Mr Everyman,' he sneered.

He aimed a right hook at Nemo's nose.

At long last Nemo reacted. Perhaps enough adrenalin had at last pooled in the bottom of Nemo's brain for him, or perhaps the poised fist of the gent prompted some subconscious trigger. Whichever it was, Nemo acted with lightning speed.

He danced.

He quickstepped to the left, shimmied to the right, and just avoided the swiftly flying fists of the gent. 'Our cover's been blown!' he yelled, his voice sounding like that of a man with a sofa's armrest crammed into his mouth.

'I *know*,' returned Thinity as she ran centrifugally round the south, east, and northern walls of the room to evade the flying fists of the two other gents.

Nemo danced out of the room. He merengued. As the gent hurled himself at him he performed a salsa figure of eight. Back in the corridor he lambada'd. He danced the *Silla Giratoria*, left foot, right foot, left foot, right foot, left foot, right foot, left foot, half turn to the left, half turn to the right, as the gent tried, with an angry expression, to seize him.

Behind him, he realised, the receptionist was waiting, her burly arms ready. Before he was even sure what was happening a pencil shot through the air like a bolt from a crossbow, to embed itself twangingly in the plaster of the wall.

Nemo danced pachanga heel taps, and executed a perfect pachanga cross swivel, before hurling himself at the door of the room that held Smurpheus prisoner. But instead of bashing through this door, as he hoped, he rebounded from it with a sore shoulder. The gent leapt at him. In a panic, Nemo danced a honky-tonk stomp, but that just meant banging his feet up and down, and didn't remove him from the scene of danger.

The gent whipped out a huge handgun, and in an instant had rammed it in Nemo's face.

Nemo, accordingly, said 'eek' on an indrawn breath. This single syllable captured precisely the quality of his high-pitched alarm.

The gun was being pressed up hard against his nose. He could feel the lips of its barrel wholly encircling the tip of his nose, squashing it against his face.

'Perhaps now, Mr *Ev*eryman,' sneered the gent, 'you *will* accept the inevitability *of* my triumph?'

With a dancing genius born of terror, Nemo *danced*. He danced a mambo el molinita, with an underarm spot turn to the right and a swivel quarter turn, lurching backwards and away from the gent and slipping past the receptionist. He jived down the corridor, pulling sharply away from the gent, who yelled in frustration.

The gent's gun was still attached to his face. He could feel the weight of it, dragging outwards by the momentum of his spin, but clamped to the lumpy end of his nose like a sucker fish. 'Hey,' objected the gent.

Nemo paso dobled (or, technically, paso singled) a few yards further down the corridor whilst trying to yank the gun from the end of his nose. It was attached tight as a sucker dart, but with one strong tug it came free. He looked up. The receptionist was advancing on him, holding a second sharpened pencil before her like a stiletto. The gent, looking mean, was running directly at him. Nothing seemed to knock off the gent's top hat. With a sense of the irrelevance of the thought, Nemo found himself wondering why that was. It was uncanny.

'Grrr,' yelled the gent. It's not an easy syllable to yell, that one, but the gent managed it.

Nemo quickstepped back, and rumba'd a few yards down the corridor. He did an alemana turn, opening out on to the left with both arms extended in a T. With an open-hip twist he brought the gun to bear on the two figures rushing up the corridor towards him.

He had never before in his life so much as touched a real gun, let alone fired one. But the situation seemed desperate. He aimed the gun as best he could, said, after a moment's pause, 'Cha-cha-cha!'

And fired.

The sound of the gunshot was like actual violence being done to Nemo's ears. To say it was deafening would give the impression that it was akin to a radio turned up too loud, a party in the next-door apartment, or a truck driving past. But it was much much louder than any of these. It seemed to shred Nemo's eardrums and leave him with only a muffled hum. The blast dazzled his eyes.

Worse, his pulling the trigger was followed by a sharp pain in his right wrist. The pain was so severe that he immediately dropped the gun. 'Bugger,' he yelled, a word which sounded faint and woolly to his own ears, although it was spoken with enough force.

He barely had time to take in the fact that a large hole had now appeared in the middle of a poster of a rabbit, from whose grinning mouth a talk-bubble announced, 'I'm A Clever Bunny Because I Brush *Twice A Day*.' There was now nothing between the rabbit's face and his fluffy feet but circular vacancy. Plaster dust was floating through the hole.

'Bugger!' yelled Nemo, holding his sore wrist in his good hand, and dancing furiously along the corridor and into the waiting room.

As he entered, all the waiting patients looked up, as one, from their magazines.

Nemo did the hockey stick, the peek-a-boo, the New York overspill and the zigzag in front of the astonished waiting patients, cursing loudly the whole time. They had heard the gunshot, and now were witnessing this gunless man come hopping and cavorting into the waiting room yowling in pain. Their faces were eloquent of thought processes concerning new developments in dental practice, and the likelihood of they themselves becoming test subjects. Nemo couldn't worry about that. His thoughts were dominated by his own pain. He had the horrible sense that he had sprained his wrist very nastily indeed. Perhaps even broken it.

The gent and the dental nurse burst from the corridor into the waiting room. The gent was holding the gun.

Nemo leapt on to the table, scattering 1970s copies of *Punch* and *Good Housekeeping* left and right and occasioning squeals from the people sitting nearby. The gent leapt from one side and the receptionist from the other, and, rapidly, but gracefully, he chicken-walked back on to the floor. There was a crash as the gent and the nurse clattered together and fell on the table.

Still holding his wrist, and still swearing, Nemo did the mashed potato, the boiled potato, the alamana turn, the Turkish towel, the lado-a-lado, the promenade, the samba whisk, the bota fogos (in the shadow position) and finally the hover corté.

The gent was aiming his gun in a considered manner directly at Nemo. Nemo stopped dancing.

'Move again *and* I will shoot,' the gent declared.

The waiting room crowd went 'Ooh!' in chorus-unity, their eyes collectively on the white-gowned gent. They swung their gaze to the poster on the far wall that read 'Be Sure To Floss, or You'll Make Your Dentist Cross!' As one, they looked back at the white-smocked gent. They looked at Nemo. He could feel the assembled gaze almost as a palpable pressure on his inflamed gums. They went 'Ooh!' again and drew back further into their chairs.

The gent stepped over to Nemo and pressed the gun into his belly. He brought his face close to Nemo's. 'Mr *Every*man,' he said. 'I represent *the* force of inevitability. Surrender *is* now *your* only option.' He smiled, evilly. 'Let us say, there are *a* few questions I should *like to* ask.'

Nemo drew a deep breath into his lungs. There was nothing for it.

He exhaled as fully as he could, breathing right into the

face of the gent. The foul stench of (simulated) years of accumulated gum decay and dental unhygiene reeked out. The gent, unprepared, could not stop himself flinching. 'It's the *smell*,' he barked, dismayed, averting his face and trying to muffle his nose with his free hand.

Nemo seized the chance. It was time for the cancan.

Nemo lashed out with his right leg, and caught his adversary exactly between his thighs, at the lowest point of his torso. The force of the kick was enough to raise the gent off the ground. Nemo dropped his right leg and swung high and strong with his left, smacking the gent in his solar plexus and propelling him spectacularly across the room.

He collided with the nurse, and swept her off her feet. Together the two figures flew clear over the reception desk, crashed through the window and plummeted the single storey to the street outside.

Nemo was breathing hard. His wrist was still very sore, but a sense of victory was taking some of the edge off the pain. He glanced behind him, where the half-dozen people waiting were staring at him.

Spontaneously they began to clap.

But there was no time to delay. The smattering applause sounded behind him as he rushed back to the corridor.

.0+I)=::

Running, he grabbed at the door frame of the room in which Thinity was fighting the two gents, and swung inside.

It was mayhem. The gents, perhaps through inefficient time-management, were attacking Thinity one after the other instead of both at the same time. Accordingly she was fighting off first one gent and then the second with her rapid-slapping hand-flapping fighting style, both her elbows tucked in at her sides and her hands moving in a blur in front of her chest. As one gent staggered back under this, the other recovered himself and leapt forward.

Nemo stepped into the room. Various dental accessories were arranged on a work surface at the side of the room; from this collection Nemo selected a broad, shallow metal pan. He hefted it in his good hand.

As the second gent staggered back and the first collected himself and launched into the fight, Nemo moved forward. He tapped the second gent on his shoulder. He looked round. With all his might Nemo swung the metal pan flat against his face.

There was a noise like a tin car colliding with a bone wall.

When Nemo pulled the pan away, the agent's face behind it was a rictus of surprise: grinning with pain, his eyes wide. As Nemo watched, his teeth peeled away from his grin one by one and fell to the floor. They dropped like unusually regular Tetris blocks, and piled irregularly on the floor.

When his mouth was wholly empty of teeth he leaned back a little way, then toppled forward. He hit the ground with a *wampum* noise and did not move.

The first gent, interrupted in the middle of his flappy-hand fighting with Thinity, looked behind him. His face contracted into a snarl, and he fished a gun from inside his jacket. Nemo could only manage a frightened smile as the gun was brought up, aimed at his head and – *crash*—

Thinity had leapt high, kicked the back of his head, and his face smashed into the little metal bowl on a stalk in which pink-tinted water gurgled continually beside the dentist's chair. 'And,' said Nemo, sagging with relief, 'rinse.'

$$^{o}\underline{\textbf{bd}}^{o}$$
$$\textbf{U}$$

There was no time to waste. Together they ran into the corridor, and shouldered the door of the adjacent room open. Once, twice, thrice they collided with it before it snapped off its lock and swayed open.

Inside Smurpheus was strapped to a dental chair. Standing over him was a white-coated elderly man with strong, handsome features. He wore a round mirror strapped to his forehead, the sort of thing dentists used to wear in the old days. There was a fat elasticated band holding this mirror in place, and above this his snow-coloured hair was abundant and white as virgin cotton, as white and pure as the advertising for low-tar cigarettes. Nemo recognised him at once, and couldn't contain himself. 'Olivier! Olivier!' he cried out. 'Never before have I asked life for more, just Olivier.' He stepped forward. 'Can I have your au'ograph? I'm a big fan.'

'Get a grip, Nemo,' said Thinity. 'He's not the *real* Olivier. Nobody here is real – haven' you fi'ured that out? He's just one more ava'ar of the *enemy*.' She seemed to be speaking more clearly, as if her gum disease were going into spontaneous remission.

Nemo looked over to Smurpheus, tied into the chair. His mouth was full of chrome. His eyes were full of pleading.

'Vat?' screeched the Olivier figure. 'Vat are you *doink*? How dare you interrupt me in ze middle of my vurk?' He stood up, brandishing the dental instruments he had been using on Smurpheus. They resembled cutlery, but it was not a close resemblance. No conventional food could ever be so tough or intractable as to need eating implements of such multi-pronged sharpness.

'Guarts!' screeched the snow-haired old gent. 'Guarts! In here at vonce!'

Thinity grabbed the circular mirror strapped to his forehead, pulled it forward and allowed it to snap back against the old man's face.

'Gott in Himmel!' he cried, flinching backwards and dropping his dental tools. He stumbled against a surface upon which was a tray of chrome picks, forks, spikes and suchlike surgical knives, knocking it on to the floor. It fell with a sustained and ear-paining series of clatters. 'Argh!' cried the dentist, hopping furiously. A short-bladed surgical device, something that looked like a chrome razor fixed to a chrome stick, had landed pointy end down on his foot, embedding itself through the material of his shoe. 'Aieee!' he shrieked, hopping and dancing on his other foot.

Thinity and Nemo stood motionless, wholly absorbed in his performance.

The evil dentist lurched across the room and smacked his face vehemently into a perspex light-box hung on the far wall; a device designed for the display of dental X-ray images. The perspex cracked and the box juddered, leaping off its hook. As the dentist reeled coltishly away, holding his nose and making *mmrf! mmrf!* noises, expressive of the pain caused by this abrupt compression of his nasal region, the light-box fell down hard on to his good foot. From the sound it made as it landed, several bones in the dentist's foot cracked with the impact, like the top of a crème brûlée under the pressure of a spoon.

Nemo wondered if the old man had exhausted his vocabulary of words with which to convey his discomfort, but at this new indignity he yelped like a puppy. He said, 'Wooah! Ow-who!' He added, 'Oo-*oo*-oo!' He saint-vitus-danced through a half-circle. He said, 'Pnargh! Pnurgh! Pnurgh!', let go of his nose and tried to lift his broken foot to his right hand. This left him, naturally, with no feet on which to stand; which in turn resulted in him falling over.

His back knocked open the room's only window, and he tumbled through, outside and down. There was a thud.

The silence in the dentist's surgery that followed had a soothing quality to it.

'Come on,' said Thinity, breaking the spell. She starting unbuckling Smurpheus from the chair.

Chapter 12

Some Peugeot 308s

One result of the interrogation that Smurpheus had endured was that he was not as coherent as he had been before. 'Let's go, Smurpheus,' said Thinity. 'We came in at the public phone across the road. We have to get you back to that node.'

'Ashle washle, murgle hooshi wooshi,' replied Smurpheus with an earnest expression on his face.

'My *Goh*,' Thinity breathed, in outrage. 'What di' they do to you?'

'Frassantossle,' replied Smurpheus.

But it was obvious what they had done. Smurpheus had had his mouth pricked, pirked, spiked, ground, jabbed, drilled, scraped, rubbed, drubbed, jellied, pumped, gnarled, puckered, cartooned, careened, zinged, duffed and carcrashed. His gums were bright red and enormously swollen. It was horrible to look upon.

Between them they lifted him from the chair and carried him out of the room, down the corridor and into the waiting room. The half-dozen patients were still sitting there, looking slightly more nervous than they had done when Nemo had first seen them. 'The den'ist,' he declared, 'will be wiv you soon.' Then Thinity and he hauled Smurpheus down the stairs and on to the street.

There was no traffic, and no passers-by. The Germanic dentist was lying face down on the pavement, not moving, although groaning a little. There was no sign either of the gent or the dental receptionist that Nemo had cancanned out of the waiting room window.

'Come on,' urged Thinity. 'Gotta get away. It won't be long before the gents arrive.'

They stepped into the road. A black Peugeot 308 sped round the corner, its engine growling angrily. It zoomed directly past them.

'Wo,' said Nemo, swaying out of the path of the vehicle.

Immediately behind came another black Peugeot 308.

It was followed by a third.

'Don't those cars look sim'lar?' said Nemo.

'Identical,' agreed Thinity. 'It means someth'in'! Déjà vu.'

The road was now filled with a constant stream of black Peugeot 308s, hurtling round the corner and rushing past them. Nemo counted twenty in as many seconds. They were driving rapidly, with barely five feet between them, and they kept on coming. There was no way Thinity and

Nemo, carrying Smurpheus, could cross the road past so relentless a flow of cars. 'Means something,' Thinity repeated.

'Means?' asked Nemo. His shoulder, wedged under Smurpheus's armpit, was starting to complain at doing its portion of supporting the slack figure of the big man. 'Can we hurry it up a li'l?' He noticed that his gums were less inflamed, and his words were coming more easily. The same seemed to be true of Thinity as well.

'Déjà vu means the program's replicatin',' Thinity explained. 'It's the vir'ual equivalent of you falling asleep at the keyboar'. Your head slumps and hits the "m" key, and suddenly you're writing mmmmmmm.' She gestured at the stream of identical cars with her free hand.

'Snurgle nurgle nurgle,' confirmed Smurpheus, threading several ccs of drool to the pavement in the process of speaking.

'One of the gents must have returned to the programming central,' Thinity said angrily, 'and set this in motion.'

The cars continued to rush by. Nemo looked nervously about him. There was no sign of any gents, but it could surely only be a matter of time before they turned up.

'We need a pelican crossing,' he said. 'Or one of those old ladies in orange with signs saying "Stop: Children". You know, a lollipop lady. Although,' he added, 'I'm not sure these cars would stop for an old woman. Or a lollipop. Or even a pelican.' After a pause, he said, 'Hey, I think my gums are wearing off – getting better, you know?'

Thinity nodded. 'They weren't programmed as a permanent addition to your avatar. They were bound to get better.'

'What?'

'We can't permanently change our representations in the McAtrix,' she answered, with a strained and hurried tone as if she resented having to explain everything to Nemo in elementary terms. 'The machines have set the parameters. The most we can do is tweak it, customise this or that for a brief period. Any change we make usually wears off after a short while.' The stream of black Peugeots continued rushing past.

'You mean,' Nemo clarified, 'any addition we make to the program when we enter the McAtrix will fade away? Any change at all?'

'Just so. Like our gums – you see, they're all better now. Same with anything.'

'My dancing ability?'

'Not that,' Thinity said crossly. 'That was uploaded directly into your brain – your real brain. Don't you remember? That's with you for ever. But superficial changes to our McAtrix avatars, they're different. Any change lasts only about half an hour. It goes away after a while, the

163

McAtrix correcting its operations. Judas,' she added, with a mournful tone, 'used to complain *most* bitterly about that. He'd program his avatar with a good head of hair, only for the hair to fall out half an hour into the mission. Came away like a sheaf of hay bursting its binding. Hair all over the floor. He used to be very peeved by that.'

Nemo considered this. 'So, for instance – your clothes?'

'These,' said Thinity, glancing down. To test her now-normal gums, she made the exaggerated *eee-aahh-ohh* movements with her lips that somebody makes after the anaesthetic has worn off. Then she sniffed dismissively through her nose, like a racehorse. 'Do you think I'd *choose* to wear this poisonous designer gear? This is the EMI's idea of clothing. And those stupid sunglasses. It's convinced that everybody should wear sunglasses, regardless of the weather. I keep throwing them away, but every time I re-enter there they are again, on my face.' She scowled. 'I tried, once, programming my own, more decent clothes for a mission. But, like Judas's hair, they simply fell off my body half an hour into the mission.'

'Fell off?' Nemo repeated. Then, to make absolutely sure he'd gotten the concept securely in his head, he said, 'Fell off? Fell away?' Then he said, 'Leaving you – naked? What, just fell off your body? Fell off completely? Off?'

She nodded sharply.

'But that's *appalling*,' Nemo said energetically. 'Naked?

Not a stitch? That's just awful.' His enthusiasm at this news indicated how very deeply he felt the awful appallingness of the contingency. There was a gleam, presumably of outrage at appallingness, in his eye. 'So they *all* fell off?' he said.

'The program rejected them,' said Thinity. 'In some senses it's like an organism, the McAtrix. It takes a little while for its programming logic to apprehend something at odds with its essential logic, but eventually it simply rectifies it.'

'But what,' Nemo said, sagging further under the weight of Smurpheus, 'about Smurpheus?'

'What about him?'

'His, nng, height? I mean, he's much taller in here than there.'

'We choose not to talk about his height,' said Thinity crossly. 'It upsets him.'

'But I don't understand. If this is a temporary adjustment to his McAtrix avatar, shouldn't he have reverted to his actual height by now?'

'Smurpheus is an exception,' Thinity declared.

'I don't understand.'

This was the straw that broke Thinity's temper. She exploded. 'You are not here to *understand*!' she cried, her voice cracking with the strain of it all. She was literally bowed down by the weight of Smurpheus. 'You are supposed to be the No One! You're supposed to be a zero – but you're not, are you? You're just a petty *someone* like everyone else in this miserable place.'

'Oh,' said Nemo, a little crushed.

'It's too awful,' Thinity cried. 'You're a weakling! You're not even supporting your half of Smurpheus's body properly. He's dragging on my neck.' With a half duck down and a heave she hauled Smurpheus's body from Nemo's grip and hoisted it into a fireman's lift across her shoulders.

'I didn't realise,' said Nemo, in a small voice.

But something had broken completely in Thinity's voice. Whatever internal dam had been holding back her anger had now been breached. 'There's no way past these cars!' she said. 'They could send a million cars along this stretch of road for all we know, and they probably will – and the *only node* out of the McAtrix for us is on the other side of the traffic.'

'Can we,' Nemo offered, hurt by her tone of voice, 'you know, go around?'

'No!' she snapped. 'No we can't! OK? Whichever road we come to, the McAtrix will have flooded it with Peugeot 308s.'

'How about getting Tonkatoi to come into the McAtrix through a different node . . . ?'

'There's no time for it. Gents will be here in *seconds*.

We're stuck. Do you really think we can outrun gents carrying a semi-conscious Smurpheus? Never. If we could just reach that node there – but we *can't*. It's over. It's useless. You understand? And do you know *why* we're in this pickle? Do you?'

'Is the answer to that,' Nemo hazarded, ' "No I don't know"?'

'That's correct, fool-boy,' she said savagely. 'I'll *tell* you why we're here. Because you were too much of a *somebody* to walk past those gents yesterday. It should have been a simple matter to slip past them, a simple matter for the No One. But that's not you, is it? You're not the No One. *Stupid* One, more like. The Idiotic One.'

Nemo's head was shrinking vertically down between his shoulders under this barrage. It was crushing. 'I'm sorry,' he said haltingly. 'I'm sorry.'

The growl of the cars had set up an almost incantatory repetitive rhythm, a *whrr-whrr, whrr-whrr, whrr-whrr*. It was an uncomfortable soundtrack to Nemo's humiliation. The breath of the vehicles' slipstream stirred his hair. Thinity's face looked strangely priest-like as her wrath and scorn poured out. The very sky seemed to have gloomed. Birds flew overhead like blown litter in the blustery air.

The endless stream of cars, the metal chant-like *whrr-whrr, whrr-whrr*.

Behind Thinity, Nemo saw a gent appear. Behind the gent was another gent. The two gents, both wearing black frock coats and top hats, were advancing towards them from the main entrance to the dentist's. Their expressions were grim. 'Thinity,' he said. 'Behind you – gents *behind* you.'

But Thinity seemed to be ignoring him. She shifted Smurpheus's supine weight across her shoulders, and took three steps along the pavement to a red post box. For a moment it looked as though she intended to stuff Smurpheus's body in the post slot. 'Of all the useless, non-No One idiots in the world, I have to get saddled with *you*,' she complained. 'What have I done to deserve this?'

Nemo felt the urgency of the situation. 'Thinity,' he called to her. 'Thinity!' He launched himself after her, but his footing was uncertain. Standing, as he had been, on the very edge of the kerb, he stumbled when he tried to push off into a run. His foot twisted on the step and his ankle gave way. Before he knew what was happening, he was staggering helplessly, flailing his arms, right into the road.

His brain spoke clearly, a death-knell sentence: *You're going to die.* It added, *In less than a second you're going to find out what it feels like to get a Peugeot 308 in the small of your back.*

Nemo did what anybody would do to protect their body,

as far as possible, from such an impact. He scrunched up his eyes.

For a moment he only stood there with his eyes closed.

Then, cautiously, he opened his eyes. He didn't risk opening them entirely. That would have been reckless. But through his half-open eyes he saw a strange sight: cars streamed away from him, like great black globs of molten plastic spat from a giant industrial manufacturing device. Identical tailgates receded, identical aerials wobbled, identical registration plates blurred, one after the other.

Slowly, Nemo turned his head to look the other way. The sight of an endless stream of Peugeot 308s hurtling directly towards him made him scrunch his eyes up again. But after a few moments, he hazarded the half-open position and saw a prospect normally enjoyed only by the wall against which crash-test dummies drive their vehicles in safety centres. Car after car boomed up towards him.

He looked down. Where the cars intersected his body something strange was happening. To Nemo's first glimpse, it looked as though his own torso had become fuzzily indistinct, hologrammatical. But when he looked again, it was the cars that became transparent, and his own body that was the only real thing. He tried to bring the image into focus, but it refused to resolve itself. It was impossible to see where ghost image and real image began or ended.

'Oh,' he said, 'Christ in a *bucket*. Thinity!'

Thinity, standing on the pavement with Smurpheus draped over her shoulders like an enormously exaggerated fox fur, was looking directly at him. 'Nemo!' she called. 'I was wrong. You *are* the No One!'

'I don't like it!' Nemo quavered. 'It's spooking me out. Thinity, help!'

But their exchange was interrupted by another voice, a penetrating and snidely evil voice. Nemo recognised it at once: the original gent, the one who had interrogated him days before, the one from the dentist. He was standing a few yards from Thinity and Smurpheus; and behind him was another gent. Two more stepped forward to take up positions immediately behind the first two.

'The famous Thinity!' called the first gent, raising his voice so that it carried over the surf of traffic. '*I* am honoured. *And* what *is* she wearing? Fox? Mink? No, I do believe it is *the* mighty Smurpheus. Two birds with *one stone*.'

Nemo was frozen with fear, flicking his glance from the four gents to the lone Thinity with her floppy burden. How could she possibly fight one gent, let alone four of them, with Smurpheus weighing her down? And yet, how could she escape? Where could she go?

Thinity, for a moment, caught Nemo's eye. She began to bend, slowly, at the knees, as if the weight of her burdens, literal and metaphorical, were finally overcoming her, and she were preparing to lay Smurpheus on the ground at the gents' feet as a spoil of war.

The first gent took a single step forward. The expression on his face was as close to triumphant as a machine could manage.

But, suddenly, Thinity straightened her legs: she leapt. With a rapidly graceful movement she put her right foot in the post slot for intermediate support and stepped neatly on to the top of the pillar box. Then, hardly pausing, she leapt into space.

Nemo's head went back trying to follow her trajectory. For a second she passed directly between him and the sun creating a localised and temporary eclipse. It was at that moment that Nemo realised what her plan was.

He didn't have time even to cry out. Thinity's designer-shod right foot, its wedge of black plastic heel and painfully tapering toe, smacked into Nemo's face. Her left foot landed on his right shoulder with bruising force.

For an instant too fleeting even to count, technically, *as* an instant (a moment of time that should more properly be described as a demiinstant, or perhaps demihemiinstant) Nemo was aware of the shocking pressure of Thinity crushing down upon him. Then the pressure lifted, granting Nemo the freedom of airway to cry out '*Oww!*' and 'oooOO!' as he started falling backwards. He had one last glimpse of Thinity, from below, as she sailed through the air over him and over the incessant cars to land safely on the far side. Then he was down.

As the back of his head struck the road he found himself in a shadowy world of holographic exhaust pipes, unreal wheels, the weirdly corrugated undersides of cars passing over him and through him. His face stung, and his shoulder felt dislocated. He was half dazed. But the backwards tumble had given him momentum to roll a little, and he slid further across the road before getting unsteadily to his feet.

He was past the flow of traffic, although only just. Wings, doors and spoilers flickered past him, centimetres from his chest. He could see the four gents on the far side of the road looking angrily at Thinity as she pressed the receiver of the public phone to Smurpheus's ear. Their anger was mingled with noncomprehension. It was plain they could not deduce how she had managed such a leap.

With an elation that only partly compensated for the battered feeling of his face and shoulder, Nemo realised that the gent could not see him at all. He truly was the No One. He had achieved it.

The gent's expression changed from angry puzzlement to a more straightforwardly angry anger. His eyes connected with Nemo's. 'Mr *Ev*eryman!' he bellowed, noticing him for the first time.

The wing mirror of the next passing Peugeot 308

clipped Nemo's left arm. It was a whumping blow, spinning Nemo through an instant half circle and tipping him away. Clutching his arm and squealing in pain he fell on the pavement at Thinity's feet.

As he struggled to get to his feet again he could see the four gents scowling at them from the other side of the interminable flow of cars. 'Come on, Nemo,' Thinity urged. 'Back through the node.'

'My arm,' he complained. 'My left arm. And my right wrist – I hurt my wrist with that stupid gun in the dentist's. And my bloody face. You trod on my face! Without so much as a by your leave! Not to mention my shoulder. And I banged the back of my head falling down—' The phone was being held against his ear as he complained, and with a tingling sensation he downloaded from the McAtrix and reappeared in the *Jeroboam*.

:+(

It was a relief to find himself back in the real world, where none of the injuries he had accrued in the McAtrix any longer applied. Indeed, when both Smurpheus and Thinity emerged from their respective chairs unharmed and unblemished, Nemo began to feel pretty smug about everything.

'What did I say?' said Smurpheus, through his unharmed real mouth. 'I *told* you that he was the No One.'

Nemo grinned. He beamed. He felt as if he were on top of the world.

'Smurpheus,' said Thinity. 'You were right; I'm sorry I doubted you. He *is* the No One.'

'Of course,' said Smurpheus complacently.

'I am, though, ain't I?' agreed Nemo. 'Blimey, fantastic. Just how *was* I able to stand in that stream of cars?'

'The system didn't recognise you. As far as the McAtrix was concerned, you'd ceased to exist. You *believed* you were the No One, and so you were.'

'You could still see me, though.'

'I,' said Thinity proudly, 'am not the system.'

'But that one car thwacked my arm with its wing mirror, didn't it?' Nemo said. '*It* treated me as real.'

'That happened when the gent recognised you. Before that moment he couldn't see you, just as the cars didn't register your presence. It was how things should have happened at the building yesterday. But then, for some reason, he saw you. Perhaps you started thinking of yourself as a Someone again.'

Nemo remembered his pride, his exhilaration, and said nothing. 'It's not easy being No One,' he said eventually, a little crestfallen.

'Still, you succeeded pretty much,' said Thinity brightly. 'Several crucial minutes of No One-ness. I'm sorry I lost my temper with you, Nemo; I'm sorry I got mad. I shouldn't have done that.'

'Hey,' said Nemo, his heart swelling. 'Think nothing of it. You know? It may have been you losing your temper that was the catalyst. May have saved all our bacon. It squashed my ego somewhat, you see, and that seemed to help my turning into the No One. I tell you what,' he added. 'The Orifice said that I'd have to choose between Smurpheus's death or my own death – but she was wrong, wasn't she? We saved Smurpheus, *and* I didn't die. She was wrong!' He felt like laughing.

Thinity walked over to him and kissed him, lightly, on the lips.

Nemo's eyes popped open. His heart bloomed, like a stop-motion film of a chrysanthemum turning from bud to bouquet. He felt a glorious sense of life flooding him. With that kiss he was alive. 'Thinity,' he said, careless of the fact that both Smurpheus and Tonkatoi were standing watching him. 'Thinity, I love you. Will you – *will* you go out with me?'

There was a moment's pause.

'Oh,' said Thinity, almost tenderly, 'of *course* not, Nemo.' She kissed him again, more lightly still. 'Of course not. Not in a million years. Sorry.'

'Oh,' said Nemo, his smile smeared stickily all over his face. 'Oh. OK.'

'I'm sorry, Nemo,' said Thinity, stepping away from him.

'No, that's all right. Sorry for. Sorry myself. I'm not too bothered, actually. You know.' There were, ridiculously, tears growing in his eyes. Inside his breast he could feel the rush of life shrink away, could feel his heart die, actually die, moment to moment, each beat like a hammer knocking in a coffin nail. It did not feel good.

'Mate,' said Tonkatoi, looking mournfully at him. 'Bummer.'

'It's OK,' said Nemo, as brightly as he could. 'Really it is.' But this was a bald lie.

'Right,' said Smurpheus. 'Let's sort out this flying submarine. After that: food. And after *that*, we need to discuss the best way to utilise our new secret weapon, the No One.'

'Righto,' said Nemo weakly.

Part 2
The McAtrix Rederided

Chapter 1

When SQUIDS **Attack**

The *Jeroboam* rattled along the old District Line, hurtling through immaculate but empty stations. Nemo sat at one of the windows, looking out. The soot-blackened walls of the tunnels, wreathed with peculiar serpentine cables and cords, fluttered past him. For one breathtaking minute the train passed from tunnel into the outer world, and Nemo could see the sunset-coloured sky above him. He looked more closely. The huge red basketball-like setting sun was reflected in the shining mosaic of tower block windows: not a single one was broken; not a single missing piece in that wine-dark jigsaw of light. What, he wondered, are the odds on that? It was hundreds of years in the future – he didn't even know how far this future was – and yet these buildings had all survived without so much as a scratch.

The red light thrown off by the enormous setting sun didn't hurt the eyes as midday sunlight would have done. Nemo stared at it for long seconds. Then the *Jeroboam* whished into a tunnel again and the windows went dark.

{[:]-)=

But Nemo was a broken man. The artificial brightness and energy of Smurpheus, Thinity and Tonkatoi only made him feel his own misery more intensely. Every time he was in close proximity to Thinity he blushed red as bleeding. It was a sort of agony. It was bad enough to have been rejected; had Nemo been able to crawl away to some pitiable hole and lie in melancholy solitude, with the salt, unplumbed and estranging sea between himself and the woman he loved so hopelessly, and nothing but a bottle of cheap brandy for company – then matters would have been bad enough. But it was much worse to have to encounter Thinity every day; to work through the usual social niceties, to say hello and goodbye, to smile when everybody smiled, and to dissemble the misery inside himself.

Thinity, meaning to be kind, made matters worse. 'You OK?' she said, the day after shredding his heart and jumping up and down on the remnants.

'Fine,' he said, beaming. 'Great! Excellent! Never better – really. Never better.'

'I'm glad to hear it,' she said.

The day after that, coming through and finding Nemo staring moodily out of the window at yet another sunset splendour of orange and gold, she had taken a seat beside him and tried to console him.

'Hey, I'm sorry,' she had said, 'if I hurt your feelings.'

Nemo tried to reply to this with a dignified, 'That's quite all right, I understand my love for you is hopeless and void, that you feeling anything at all for me is an utter impossibility, please leave me alone in my philosophical isolation to contemplate the barrenness of the cosmos.' In the event he didn't quite manage to say this. Instead he said: 'It's aw-aw,' and stopped. Then he tried again, 'It's aw-aw.' Then he sniffed noisily, pressed his eyeballs with the heel of his hand, one after the other, to try and squeeze away tears. Then he looked more intently at the view from the window as the submatrain careered into another tunnel. A voice was chanting in his head: *Pathetic!* It was saying. *Pathetic!*

'I know it's hard,' she said, with a pained expression that might have been trying to convey her empathy with Nemo's sufferings. Nemo wished she wouldn't try to convey her empathy with his sufferings. His dearest wish – or his second dearest wish (since his first involved Thinity changing her mind about him and pulling off her sweater) – was for her to go away and leave him alone. But he couldn't say this; and he couldn't find solitude in the narrow compartments of the *Jeroboam*.

He dreamt about her every night.

'Would it be possible,' Nemo suggested the following morning, 'to – you know. Upgrade my fighting ability.'

'Nemo, I won't lie to you,' Smurpheus said severely. 'Judas was our expert in uploading skills.'

'Ah. You mean, I'm stuck at the level of dancing, rather than fighting?'

'Your dancing was quite effective, I thought,' said Thinity.

It was still ridiculously painful to Nemo even to talk straightforwardly to Thinity. It was crazy. It was absurd. He needed to be stronger. He girded his metaphoric loins, smiled back and said, 'Right, right,' breezily. 'Yes, I guess so, ahhhh.' This last word was the start of a sob, which drew out for almost a second before Nemo clamped down on it. He smiled bravely with glittering eyes.

The others looked at him queerly for a moment.

'I'll 'ave a go, owi?' said Tonkatoi. 'But it's a tricky process, uploading fighting skills.'

'Don't mean to be a bother,' said Nemo in a small voice.

''Sowi,' said Tonkatoi. 'Only you got to understand, Judas was expert – expert – at packing a complex zip-complete set of coordination programs directly into the hindbrain. I'll have to do it piece by piece, build it up over time.'

'I see,' said Nemo. 'I suppose it'll be better than nothing, though, eh?'

'If you like. Come on through.'

..ooOO80Ooo..

Nemo unbuttoned the flap at the back of his pants, took his place in the chair and resigned himself to yet another insertion. Tonkatoi sat in the control seat, fussing over the machinery. ''Sall Judas's stuff, y'know?' he said. 'I'm not too familiar with it. But I'll start with some basic fighting skills.' He pulled down what looked like an eight-track cartridge marked 'Playground: Primary' and fed it into a Cherie-Blair-mouth-style slot.

Nemo's eye's widened once again as the probe went in, and for long seconds he felt the sputtering, fax-like sensation of data buzzing up his spine. He squeezed his eyes shut as the sensations accumulated unpleasantly, like nausea building towards the purgative vomit, and then, suddenly, he felt the probe being withdrawn, and he opened his eyes.

The upload machine was on fire. Tonkatoi was hopping from foot to foot and trying to beat out the fire with the sleeve of his jumper. This meant that the sleeve of his jumper also started burning. 'Oi!' he was calling. 'No!'

A fire alarm was sounding in the compartment. It acted as fire alarms have always done: to add aural panic to the physical panic of proximity to a fire, and thereby make it harder to concentrate on the job of putting the fire out.

Smurpheus and Thinity came hurrying through. The flames were leaping from Judas's console and blackening the ceiling. It occurred to Nemo (he was not sure why he had this thought at this particular time, but nevertheless) that the flames were the *exact opposites* of icicles. Icicles hang down, where these flames leapt up; icicles are cold, where these flames were evidently very hot; and icicles are frozen and immobile, where these indulged in fantastically wriggly motion. He could not imagine a more perfect mirror image of icicles, try as he might. Tonkatoi was copying the flames, insofar as he was dancing energetically with an upward-hanging fringe of fire on his sleeve. 'Oi!' he said. 'No! Oh!'

Thinity, hefting a fire extinguisher, pointed it at Tonkatoi. She depressed the button and, in an eyeblink, provided herself with a teetering white Father-Christmas-style beard. Accordingly, she cried out in her own alarm and surprise, and dropped the extinguisher. Smurpheus picked it up, swivelled it through a half turn, and pressed the button again. A plume of foam leapt through the air and affixed itself to Tonkatoi's arm. Smurpheus re-aimed and extinguished the fiery equipment.

The alarm stopped. For moments there was silence. The flying submatrain rattled through Mornington Crescent.

'@'

'That,' said Tonkatoi, as they were all recovered afterwards, 'wasn't ideal. I think I polarised the reversality.
Inadvertent, like.'

'How's your arm?' asked Thinity as she wiped her chin
clean of foam.

'Owi,' he replied.

'Did you manage to teach Nemo advanced fighting
skills?' Smurpheus asked.

Tonkatoi looked despondent. 'Look, it's really *hard*,
owi? I'm not supposed to be the geezer doing the uploads,
am I? That's Judas's job, innit?'

'Did you manage to teach Nemo any fighting skills at
all?' Smurpheus pressed.

'Basic playground,' said Tonkatoi breezily.

'Secondary playground? Or *primary* playground?'

'Primary.'

'So, as I understand it,' said Nemo, 'I have been uploaded with fighting skills such that a primary schoolboy
might deploy in the school playground.'

All three of the *Jeroboam* crew nodded in unison.

'Will that,' he said, 'be any use in a gent-fighting situation?'

They all shook their heads.

'Right,' said Nemo.

*****

'It is clear what we must do,' Smurpheus announced. 'Nemo is a weapon that can win us this war against the EMIs.'

'Agreed,' said Thinity.

'Oh,' said Nemo. 'Are you sure? I mean, I don't want to sound defeatist, but.' He considered. 'Well, I wonder if I wouldn't lead everybody to a defeat. So perhaps I do mean to be defeatist. But not in a bad way.'

'You are the No One,' said Smurpheus simply. 'We can do nothing more from within the *Jeroboam*. Judas has abandoned us. His machinery is broken. You must go back into the McAtrix as you are – do you understand? You must return to the Orifice. You must ask her for directions—'

'Directions?'

'Directions to the source,' said Smurpheus. 'Directions to the Designer of Designers, to the evil genius who created the McAtrix. Only by confronting him will you be able to bring this war to an end.'

'Righto,' said Nemo, trying to give the word a hopeful inflection.

'And we must end the war, Nemo,' Smurpheus said. 'Syon Lane is under direct threat. The EMIs have already captured me and tried to extract the information from me to get to it. When they do obtain that information, from whichever source – when they learn its location relative to their own system, they'll tunnel through and smash it. Smash it!'

'That would be a shame.'

'Shame,' said everybody, nodding ponderously.

'But they didn't learn the location from you, though,' Nemo said. 'Did they, Smurpheus?'

Smurpheus looked fiercely at the wall to his side. 'Of course not,' he said.

'Did they?' Nemo pressed.

'No. No. No,' said Smurpheus, in three separate sentences. 'Honestly.' He added, in a quieter voice, 'Obviously I can't remember *too* much. But I'm ninety per cent sure. Seventy per cent sure, and twenty per cent half-sure. Or, no – more like, sixty-five per cent sure, nineteen per cent half sure, one per cent quarter sure, and fifteen, or more precisely *fourteen*, per cent uncertain the *other* way, with the remainder . . .'

'So what you're saying is . . .' began Nemo.

But he was interrupted by a yell from Tonkatoi: 'SQUID attack!'

'Action stations!' bellowed Smurpheus, seemingly relieved that his conversation with Nemo had been interrupted. 'Let's go. Tonkatoi, divert the sub through . . . where are we now?'

'Goodge Street,' Tonkatoi yelled back.

'Turn at Tottenham Court Road, head for Holborn and

double back at Covent Garden and turn east.' He leapt up and ran out of the compartment.

Suddenly the submatrain lurched and screeched. Nemo looked up to see several globular tentacled *somethings* banging against the window. The metallic sheen of their bulbous bodies, and the sinuous rattling of their tentacles, was terrible to behold. Nemo screeched like a macaw (rather belying his self-declared reputation for bravery) and leapt back from the glass. On all sides, he saw, as he reeled around the submatrain, monstrous robotic squids were clattering against the windows and trying to force open the doors.

'Hold tight,' screamed Tonkatoi from the driver's cabin.

The train lurched abruptly to the right. SQUIDS were scattered from the left side of the train like water droplets from a shaking dog. But on the other side more of the devices clung to the fabric of the train.

Thinity sprinted through, and tossed a long stick to Nemo. 'Use this,' she yelled, 'if they get inside the compartment.' She continued running.

'What is it?' he asked. 'Laser rifle? Electro-crackle gun?' But as he called to her he looked down, and he could see it was a plain iron crowbar.

Thinity had gone.

He hefted the crowbar, steeled himself, and made his way towards the side of the submatrain still covered with

SQUIDS. One of the things had managed to squeeze open a door and insert a tentacle. In addition to the rushing and whining noises made by the train hurtling through the tunnel, the occasional clanks and bangs, Nemo could hear a weird high-pitched whistling noise, a sort of monstrous cooing or singing. With a stomachly lurch he realised it was proceeding from the mouthparts of the SQUID. They weren't attractive mouthparts, looking as they did as if they were designed for rending flesh. Nemo found himself wondering why they'd given a robot hunter-seeker mouthparts in the first place, but none of the answers he came up with reassured him in the slightest.

Suddenly the submatrain door was wrenched open a foot, a yard, and the SQUID got three more tentacles and the front of its body section inside.

Nemo thwacked it with his crowbar. It shrieked and tumbled back into the darkness, and other SQUIDS squirmed and crawled over the windows towards the partially open door. Nemo, positively yelping with fear, hauled the twin doors shut, and started banging the insides of the windows with his crowbar. He did this because he couldn't think of anything else to do, but it seemed to be effective. The SQUIDS shuddered and scuttled, several falling off. The submatrain took another sharp corner, and the remaining few scattered.

For long moments Nemo stood, holding his crowbar in

front of him and breathing heavily. He did not notice when Thinity came into the compartment until the moment when she placed her hand upon his shoulder.

'You OK?'

'That,' he said, 'was fairly frightening. Does it happen often?'

'From time to time,' she said. 'But we've found that the best defence against them is the EMP.'

'EMP?'

She patted the crowbar in Nemo's hand. 'Elementary Metal Pole,' she said. 'They don't like it up 'em. Or brought down sharply from above. They really don't. Jars them, I reckon.'

+0/0->

'Nemo,' said Smurpheus. 'You must go into the McAtrix, and visit the Orifice now.'

'Must I?' said Nemo.

'Yes. We will insert you into the McAtrix, and you will find her in a certain shop selling maps of the stars' homes.'

'Right, OK. Good, actually. Well I've a notion to give her a piece of my mind. Telling me I had to choose between you dying and my dying. Telling me I wasn't the No One, when it turns out I *am*. What kind of a prophetess is she?'

'We need her advice badly,' said Smurpheus. 'The news

from Syon Lane is distressing. The Council of Wrinklies suspects the EMIs are trying to tunnel out of their system so as to be able to attack Syon Lane. We must counter-attack at once.'

'Right,' said Nemo resolutely.

'And to that end,' added Thinity, 'we need to know how best to use your special skills.'

'Oh, well, no – really,' said Nemo, his mouth seeming to fill with glue as he tried to look her in the eye. 'Sure, whatever.' He felt a powerful urge to dig a hole, get into it, and then pull the dirt over on top of himself. Unrequited love is a miserable thing.

Chapter 2

The Orifice Revisited

Nemo found himself, once more, propelled into the McAtrix. He stepped away from the phone booth as the litter and dead leaves slowly settled to the ground. It occurred to him that whenever they entered the McAtrix they always seemed to arrive just as a miniature whirlwind was dying down. Puzzling.

He walked swiftly, making sure not to tread on the cracks in the pavement. It was no good. He couldn't bear life aboard the *Jeroboam* now that Thinity had made her feelings plain. His heart was dead and rotting inside him. Thinity hated him. She must hate him, or she wouldn't have crushed his hopes so brutally. Didn't she realise how much he loved her?

He stopped outside a shop selling maps of the stars' homes, looked up and down the street with a heavy expression and pushed the door open. Inside, a middle-aged East Asian man was standing with his arms by his side. He looked somehow familiar, but Nemo couldn't quite place his face.

'Good evening!' he announced brightly. 'You are Nemo?'

'That's me. I'm looking for the Orifice, don't know if you can help.'

The man trotted over to Nemo, still smiling, and stood before him. Suddenly he flicked out his hand: the palm slapped noisily against Nemo's cheek, stinging him. In a swift motion, the man took two steps back and folded his arms in front of him. 'Ow!' Nemo called out, his own hand going to the spot where he had been hit. 'What'd you do *that* for?'

'Ah,' said the man. 'I had to make sure you are who you *say* you are.'

'By slapping me?'

'You do not really know somebody unless you fight them.'

'And that counts as fighting, does it?'

'Close enough.'

'You don't know someone till you fight them?' Nemo shrilled, still rubbing his cheek. 'What *on earth* does that mean? You're saying that a person is more intimately acquainted with some bloke they got drunk with and thwacked in a pub car park than with their best friend of twenty years?'

'Indeed,' said the strange man. 'You *must* slap your friend. From time to time. To maintain intimacy.' He bowed.

'You're a major loon,' Nemo opined.

The man did not seem bothered by this judgement. 'I will,' he said, 'take you to the Orifice now.'

Still rubbing his cheek, Nemo said, 'Well, all right, thank you.'

'This way.' The man was pointing at a door in the corner of the shop, on which was the CLUEDO™ logo, and a sign saying 'SECRET PASSAGEWAY'. 'This direction, if you please,' said the man. 'Step through the Mr Benn door.'

'Mr Benn door?' queried Nemo.

But the man had opened the door and stepped through into a bright-lit corridor. Nemo followed.

[:=|]

The two of them walked a little way along a nondescript corporate-looking corridor. 'This is a secret passageway, isn't it?' Nemo panted. 'It was the fact that the door had a sign on it saying "secret passageway" that gave it away.'

'This way, please,' said the hyperpolite gentleman, opening a second door on to what looked like a school playground. 'The Orifice will see you now.'

'You're the Orifice's – what? Guardian? Manservant?'

The man smiled, and stepped through. As Nemo followed he was startled by a loud distinctively female yell. The Orifice, displaying an agility that belied her apparent age, had leapt from behind the open door and smacked her manservant on the side of the head with a gracefully managed karate kick. The recipient tumbled down, screaming, tried to roll with the fall and get to his feet, his arms in front of him karate style.

As Nemo watched, boggling, the Orifice slammed him with a left, slammed him again with a right, and finally smacked him so that he fell backwards over a wooden bench. He was lying motionless.

The Orifice stepped over him. 'That's much better,' she said, indulgently. 'You're getting better all the time, Kato. Reflexes much improved.'

The heap of humanity lying on the concrete moaned something that might, perhaps, have been, 'Thank you, ma'am.'

'Why did you do that?' asked Nemo, stepping forward. 'You just punched his lights out. I thought he was your manservant. Was he an enemy in disguise?'

The Orifice was closing the door behind Nemo. 'Enemy? Not at all. Don't you worry about Kato there. It's a sort of game we play. Look on it as a kind of training. The McAtrix is a dangerous place these days. I'm trying to hone his responses.'

'That's a pretty savage honing,' said Nemo.

'You must be,' said the Orifice, 'the only person in the world not to have seen the Pink Panther movies.'

'I'm phobic about the colour pink,' said Nemo. 'Brings me out in hives.'

'Come,' said the Orifice, beaming at him. 'Sit, sit.'

Glancing again at the groaning heap of the floored Kato, Nemo lowered himself on to the bench. He found himself in an urban schoolyard: a small concrete ground between three high walls. Low cross-barred goalmouths were painted on two opposite walls, and goalies' areas were painted on the floor; but the paint was old and scuffed and could barely be made out. Beyond a wire-mesh fence Nemo could see a deserted stretch of road, with a discount sofa warehouse over the way. Some pigeons pecked at the leftover crumbs of packed lunches. The door he had come through was revealed now as the fire escape to a tall brick building. Nobody was about but he himself, the Orifice and the still moaning Kato on the floor.

'So,' he said. 'Here we are.'

'Here we are indeed,' said the Orifice.

There was an awkward pause.

'So,' said Nemo. He cleared his throat. 'And how are you?'

'Fine,' said the Orifice.

'Good,' said Nemo.

There was another awkward pause.

'Was there some particular reason you wanted to see me?' said the Orifice, eventually.

'Well,' said Nemo, shifting on the bench a little. 'Well, what it is, is – well. Look. Put it like this. Um. You told me I *wasn't* the No One.'

The Orifice nodded.

'I'm not one to complain,' said Nemo, 'but it, sort of, turns out I *am* the No One after all. I stood in a stream of Peugeot 308s, and it didn't hurt even a little bit. It was most disconcerting.'

'Congratulations,' said the Orifice, rather smugly.

This stoked up Nemo's outrage a notch or two. 'Now look,' he said. 'As I say, I'm not one to complain. Only you *definitely* told me I wasn't, and it turns out I was. Am. In addition to which, you said – I remember this distinctly – that a situation would arise in which I would have to choose between my death and Smurpheus's. You said I was going to be given a choice, let Smurpheus die and carry on living myself; or die myself to save Smurpheus.'

'And?'

'And I'm still alive, aren't I!'

'Are you complaining about that?'

'Not complaining about *that*,' said Nemo. 'No. I'm worried about the accuracy of your prophecies. You're supposed to know the future. But what you said didn't happen.'

'Didn't it?'

Nemo put both his palms up in front of his chest, which was his own just-invented sign language for 'of course not, I'm still alive aren't I?'

'You crossed the river of cars,' said the Orifice. 'You returned to the real world.'

'And I *didn't die*, and neither did Smurpheus, that's my point. You said that either the one or the other would happen, and neither did.'

'So, let me ask you: what happened,' purred the Orifice, 'when you asked Thinity to go out with you?'

Nemo paused. 'That doesn't count.'

'Wasn't that a sort of death?'

'Oh,' said Nemo, losing his rag, or at least misplacing it momentarily. 'That's so *lame*. You didn't say that I ran the risk of a metaphorical death resulting from a disappoint-ment in my love life, you said I was really going to die. Not "die inside", *actually* die. You really had me going. I was scared. Really, very.'

The expression on the Orifice's face was placid and implacable. 'I can't help how you choose to interpret my words. You need to pay attention to an oracle if you want to follow her advice. Read between the lines. Didn't you ever see *Macbeth*?'

'Are you saying that you were deliberately trying to mislead me?' said Nemo, growing heated. 'Like a cryptic crossword?'

'Not at all. I was playing the game. This is how the game is played.'

'The game?'

'This is how celebrities speak: politicians, movie stars, famous people. Have you ever known a politician, movie star or celebrity give a straight answer to a question? Of course not. And I'll tell you why: because celebrity is about evasion. A celebrity is somebody evading the fundamental truth – that they don't matter. Nobody matters. Everybody exists, nobody has value. Eventually the sun will explode and swallow the earth. Eventually the universe will die a cold death. What will celebrity matter then? Nothing. In order to inhabit celebrity it is necessary to avoid this truth, or else it corrodes your fame. Hence double-talk.'

'Politicians,' Nemo said cautiously, 'maybe. But celebrities in general? Are they so evasive? I'm not convinced.'

The Orifice clucked, a noise like two billiard balls colliding. 'They'll say *we're very much in love, I'm wearing a vial of my life-partner's blood around my neck to signify our eternal connection*, and three months later they're both with other people. They'll say *it was a joy and a pleasure working with X*, when what they mean is *I hate him, he stole my limelight, I wish he were dead*. They'll say *before I collect this award I'd like to thank the following people*, when what they mean is *Me! Me! I did it! My glory!*'

'I really,' said Nemo, his annoyance shifting into a kind

of desperate pleading, 'I *really* don't understand. Can you just tell me what is going on? What *are* you, anyway?'

'What am I?' said the Orifice pleasantly. 'What do you think?'

'I think you're the sort of person who'll never answer a question with an answer when they can answer it with another question.'

She nodded at this. 'And?'

'I think you're a program. Not a person, one of the EMIs.'

'Nearly right,' said the Orifice, still smiling. 'I straddle the two worlds, if you like. I'm the link, the opening through which each can reach each.'

'Right,' said Nemo. After a pause, he added, 'Which means?'

'Which means that I can help you. Do you want to know how to defeat the EMIs, to preserve Syon Lane?'

'Obviously,' said Nemo. 'Although—'

'Although?'

'Well, whilst I'm obviously keen to, you know, what you said. Help humanity win the war and all that. But at the same time—'

The Orifice smiled a Gioconda smile. Or, to be precise, it was a slightly more predatory expression. More ana-conda than Gioconda. 'What?'

'Well, obviously it'd be a good thing if . . . defeating the

EMIs and so on. But I can't say that I'm really in this for military reasons. I'm more concerned with, well, you know.'

'Thinity.'

'Yes, Thinity.'

'I see,' said the Orifice benignly.

'Only,' said Nemo, hope spurting in his heart and giving his words a wheedling, slightly desperate edge, 'only, if you meant what you said about wanting to *help* me . . .'

She was looking away. Kato, behind them both, was getting slowly to his feet. 'Yes,' she said. 'I can help you, Nemo. You are in love with Thinity. That is, in itself, a significant thing. Yet she does not love you. It is a dilemma. Only one person can solve this dilemma.'

'Who? Who's the one person?'

'Why, the person who designed the McAtrix. The Designer. You must go and see him.'

'And how will I find him?'

'You need the device.'

'Device?' Nemo pressed. 'What device?'

'A device with which you can plot your path to the Designer,' she replied simply. 'The device of plot. This device is currently in the ownership of a very old, very powerful program called the Frurnchman. He has been inside the McAtrix for an awfully long time. Longer than any of us.'

'And where does he live?'

'In the EMI tower. Your friends know where that is. Once you have located the device, you will be able to confront the Designer.'

'And that will win me Thinity?'

'It could,' she said. 'Of course, it's a zero sum thing. Thinity must die for Thinity to live. She must pass away for you to win her.'

'Aoow,' Nemo whined, high-pitched. 'What's *that* supposed to mean? Is it another of your *Macbeth*y prophecy things? Thinity must pass away for me to win Thinity – can't you be more precise than that? Am I going to get her or not?'

'Sorry kiddo,' she said. She patted his knee.

'I love her,' Nemo blurted, tears surprising his eyes and growing sticky like runny eggs on his hot cheeks. 'I really love her! I can't bear it! I want her so much . . .'

But the Orifice was getting creakily to her feet. Kato had opened the fire escape and she was shuffling towards it. 'Time for me to go. You can never see past the prophecies you don't understand.'

'Well of *course* you can't,' said Nemo, jumping to his feet and rubbing his face with the cuff of his jacket. 'That goes without saying. Why not give me a prophecy I *do* understand? Then I *could* see past the prophecy and know what's going to happen.'

The Orifice paused on the threshold of the open door and looked back at Nemo. 'Next time you're in the real world, take a good look.'

'A good look at *what*?' Nemo snapped in a crotchety-adolescent tone of voice, tears hemming his words.

'I don't know. The sky. The sun. Just take a good look around. The answers are there, if you look. It's the obvious stuff, the stuff you're not even noticing.'

And she stepped inside, and was gone.

(8-|)=[

The door clicked shut.

For long minutes Nemo simply stood, gathering himself. The crying thing had shaken him, and it took a while to retrieve his composure. After his breathing had returned to normal, and his eyes had cooled, Nemo realised that he didn't know how to get out of the McAtrix. He had, he knew, to go back through the same node through which he had entered; but he had no idea where that was, in relation to his present location. 'I should,' he said, 'have gone through the Mr Benn door with those two.'

But it was too late to worry about that now.

'What to do?' Nemo wondered aloud. He looked around for a phone, although he wasn't sure whom he might call. There was a rustle in the air as the flock of pigeons that had been strutting around the yard bickered into flight; and through the mess and struggle of wings Nemo saw a gent striding purposefully towards him.

'Mr *Ev*eryman,' boomed the gent. 'We meet again.'

'Oh,' said Nemo, his stomach fluttery, 'oh blimey O'Reilly.'

'You are *an* elusive individual, Mr *Ev*eryman. But I am nothing *if* not persistent.'

Nemo's heart was staggering in his chest like a lamb's first efforts at walking. He tried to steel himself. It's OK, he thought. I've been uploaded with more than dance now. I can fight, albeit at a rudimentary level. The thing to do, he addressed himself, is to take the initiative. But this is a gent! he countered internally. I can't fight a gent. I've only been uploaded with basic primary-level playground fighting. But, he insisted, this is a playground. As this internal dialogue batted back and forth across the lobes of his brain, Nemo stood indecisively biting his lip. *Go on, go for him*, said one internal voice. *Run for it*, counselled the other. *Oh for crying out loud*, came a third voice. *Will you two stop arguing?*

A pigeon flapped across the yard, nearly collided with the gent, lurched in midair and careered towards Nemo. He reflexly put up a hand to defend himself and the pigeon flapped spastically in front of his face, before swivelling in the air again and flying straight up with strong strokes. Nemo had a vivid afterimage of thrashing wings, of reptilian feet hanging in flight, of blank eyes, but also of the prism light tangled in the creature's breast feathers.

'Mr *Every*man,' the gent was saying. 'This charade *has* gone on long enough. It is time *to* draw it to an end.'

Nemo made his decision.

He leapt forward and ran straight at the gent, screaming. 'Yaaaaah!' he cried. And saw a momentary look of surprise twist almost to fear on the gent's face. Then Nemo shouldered into him, knocking him down. Nemo leapt over the supine gent and carried on running. He couldn't help himself: now he was going 'Woo!-woo!' and running around the perimeter of the playground.

The gent got quickly to his feet.

Nemo forced himself to stop running, and to stop whooping. But his feet felt alive. He slow-shoe shuffled a couple of steps, and then began the beguine. 'Yaah!' he called again in derision.

'You leave me no option,' said the gent severely.

He reached up with both hands, took hold of the top of his top hat and pulled down. The barrel of the hat sank down, like a piston. The gent released it and it popped up again.

Nemo, tap-dancing on the spot, watching with interest.

There was a pop, and a sudden rush of wind, and a second, identical gent was standing next to the first. The only difference between this simulacrum and the original was a blue band around the top hat, upon which was written the legend 'CTRL-P'. Nemo didn't have time to wonder what this device signified, because both gents were pulling down the barrels of their hats and, with double pop and a larger swirl of air, two more gents appeared.

The four turned themselves into eight.

The eight turned themselves into sixteen.

'Wow,' said Nemo, as the breeze died down again.

'Mr *Ev*eryman,' these sixteen gents said in unison. 'Now it is time *to* give *you* a pasting.'

'Pasting,' said Nemo. 'Oh.'

The original gent, the only one whose top hat was not adorned with a CTRL-P band, stepped to the front. He raised his arm. 'On my command,' he shouted, 'we will bundle.'

The mass of gents tensed in readiness.

'Bundle!' yelled the first gent.

In an instant all the gents had leapt on top of Nemo. He was squashed to the ground under a heaving mass of bodies. It was, he reflected, only too accurate a symbol of his entire life. Everything was getting on top of him, both literally and metaphorically. Everything. His job was rubbish. His social life was nonexistent. Then Tori Amos got married to a sound engineer rather than to him (or even to no one, which would at least have allowed him still to dream). Then he discovered that his whole existence was an EMI-created sham, nothing more than a computer program. The upside there, of course, was that he had met Thinity: but – fate hurling elephant-sized chunks of misery down upon him from above – Thinity wanted nothing to do with him. And now he was being literally squashed to death by sixteen simulacra of police-program gents in top hats and frock coats. It was, he thought, bitterly ironic. Possibly ironic, if he'd been able to pinpoint what the irony was, precisely. Or, indeed, if he'd had a clear notion in his head of what irony was, exactly, and the ways it differed from sarcasm, metaphor and litotes.

He couldn't breathe.

'Mr *Ev*eryman,' said sixteen identical gents simultaneously, above him and all around. 'We *are the* force of inevitability, and we are about *to* squash you *like* a bug.'

'Great,' gasped Nemo with compressed lungs. Things could hardly get any worse. He was about to die an ignominious death. He would never see Thinity again. It was unbearable.

But then, miraculously, he felt the pressure ease from his squashed body. There was a clatter as the pile sagged, and the gents fell to the floor. But Nemo was getting to his feet, rising through the very bodies of his enemies. It was a strange thing: his viewpoint passed through a confusion of inner and outer, the black cloth of the gents' clothing, the shadowy red and mauve of inner organs where blood pulsed and swirled, the dense ivory-coloured bars of bones, all panning down through Nemo's vision as he stood up. The pile of gents was taller than he, so for one disorienting moment when he stood upright he was faced with a dark blur. He moved a little to the right, into a vaguely lit spongy something. The gent whose inner organs he was seeing moved his head and called out: a flutter of teeth glinted, the intestinal curl of tongue muscle vividly red in naked light, darkened almost at once as the gent closed his mouth again.

Nemo took two long strides and was free of the whole heap of gentness.

He looked behind him at the struggling heap of now infuriated gents. They were disentangling themselves, with some awkwardness, from one another and looking angrily around. Nemo didn't stop. His invisibility had not lasted very long the last time he had achieved it, and there were no guarantees it would last any longer this time. He hurried round them and walked straight through a brick wall, his sight blurring brown before being dazzled by interior striplights. He was in a well-lit school corridor, and he ran hurriedly down this and through a closed double door. Rows of schoolchildren in their tiny desks were bending their attention upon a teacher, who was writing something in chalk upon a blackboard. Hurrying past, Nemo caught a glimpse of this inscription. It was 'WE ARE ALL HUMAN'. It was, Nemo thought, a strange thing to write on a classroom blackboard. But he couldn't loiter.

With a strobing flicker of dark and light Nemo passed through the exterior wall and on to a small patch of lawn. What should he do? Where to go? It was hopeless. This No One invisibility, walk-through-solid-objects business was good for avoiding gents, sure: but could he turn it off? How would he eat? If he gobbled a scone would it drop straight to the floor? How could he even pick it up to eat it?

He was just beginning to panic when he heard a deep-thrumming voice behind him. 'Hello, Nemo.' It was Smurpheus.

Chapter 3
The Frurnchman

'It wasn't easy to track you,' Smurpheus told him as he led him back to the new portal he had created two blocks from the school. 'The Orifice's assistant led you many miles away from your original entry point. But luckily, even though the gents cannot see you, we can.'

'They jumped on top of me,' said Nemo, gasping. 'Dozens of them. They pulled down on their hats, and somehow—'

'Hats?' queried Smurpheus. 'They wear no hats. That is simply the shape and colour of the tops of their heads.'

This pulled Nemo up short. 'You're kidding,' he said. 'That's pretty strange.'

'It is how the Designer designed them. What you took for hats are in fact large buttons, to be depressed for the reason you saw. But there is no time to loiter here: we must return to the *Jeroboam*.'

Nemo picked up the phone and left the McAtrix.

€:•)

'What I don't understand,' said Nemo, getting up from the chair, 'is how I don't just fall through the floor. When I become the No One, I mean. It seems I can pass through everything else.'

'Because of who you are,' said Smurpheus, doing up his trousers and simultaneously slipping into one of his pompously vatic moods. 'You are the No One. The McAtrix, built upon celebrity and consumption, does not recognise you; the hollow people, the hollow buildings—'

'—the hollow Peugeots,' Nemo interjected, nodding.

'But the earth!' Smurpheus boomed, 'Is! Not! Hollow! It supports *all* life, even the pure No One life you have achieved. It supported life for millions before celebrity, logos and consumerism spread its plague through humanity.'

'Right,' said Nemo. 'OK. Great. Fantastic. That makes it a *lot* clearer. Although I suppose, if I'm being honest,' he began to add, as his natural urge to gabble started to kick in, 'I can't say I entirely follow the logic. If that were the case, I should surely sink through the pavement, you know? Go at least ankle deep. But I don't, at all. It's as if I'm the No One horizontally but not vertically.'

'I have already explained,' said Smurpheus, looking haughty.

'But I'm just thinking about your explanation,' said Nemo. 'And I'm not sure it makes sense. The earth? The earth isn't any more real than anywhere else inside the McAtrix, is it? I mean, it's all false, all illusion.'

'All right then, Mr I-suddenly-know-everything-about-the-McAtrix,' snapped Smurpheus, giving up a good proportion of his *gravitas* in order the more effectively to express his annoyance. 'How do you explain it?'

'*I* don't know,' said Nemo defensively. 'Maybe if I knew more about the rationale behind the whole No One thing. Is it something programmed? Because if so, it must be that whoever programmed it wants me to be able to pass through walls but not through the ground, or at least—'

Thinity had come into the room. Nemo's words dried. He felt his face become a piece of sunset-based conceptual art.

'Hi Nemo,' she said, brightly.

Her words were like swords to him. 'Hi,' he mumbled in return, like a teenager. He turned his head away, as if her beauty were the glare of the sun and might damage his retinas.

'What's up?'

'Nemo has encountered the Orifice,' declared Smurpheus. 'She has instructed us to seek the Frurnchman.'

'He's got a device,' said Nemo, still looking at the wall. 'Apparently.'

'Using this device,' boomed Smurpheus, 'we can plot a path to the Designer himself.'

Thinity's voice shifted into a more hushed, more awe-y tone. 'The Designer? Nobody can access the Designer, surely. He is inaccessible.'

'Nemo can,' said Smurpheus confidently.

'This is *so* great,' Thinity said. 'If you can get to the Designer . . .'

'. . . you can end this war,' Smurpheus said. 'Exactly.'

'Victory!' said Thinity.

'I'll do my best,' Nemo mumbled. 'But I don't know how I'll be able to end the war all by myself.'

'If you can get us into the Designer's office,' said Smurpheus, 'Thinity and I will . . . persuade him . . . to call off his SQUIDS. Now let us sleep, and gather our energies. When we awake, we will go back into the McAtrix – and end this war finally and for all time.'

*[[[[|8>)]=

The others settled into their cubbyholes; except for Tonkatoi, who was steering the train and keeping a lookout for SQUIDS. But Nemo, though he was tired, could not sleep. His head was racing faster than the submatrain in which he sat, staring through the windows.

The train rattled along the District Line, passing in and out of tunnels. Once again, the real sky was sunset red. It always seemed to be sunset in the real world, Nemo thought idly. Always a fat red sun sitting on the horizon. Always the sky apricot and plum and tomato, with orange clouds like rags. It was certainly beautiful. He wondered whether there was some time dilation effect of being inside the McAtrix that meant he always seemed to emerge at dusk.

But that wasn't what his mind was truly concerned about. He could only think of Thinity, of how much he loved her, and how hopeless his love was. Some part of his mind offered optimism, like a faded bunch of flowers: *Maybe, if you lead them to the Designer and they end the war . . . maybe she'll be so impressed with you that . . . maybe she'll be so grateful for what you've done that . . .*

But he knew it didn't work like that. Thinity simply didn't feel anything for him. That was all there was to it. What was it the Orifice had said? Nemo would have to lose Thinity to gain Thinity. But he couldn't work out what that meant in real terms. But the first part, the losing Thinity part, chimed real enough in his heart.

}:-ε

Smurpheus came blundering through. 'Terrible news,' he announced. 'Syon Lane is under attack! The EMIs are digging a new tunnel, from Richmond, under the dried-out river bed.'

'Digging a new tunnel?'

'They'll be in Syon Lane in six hours.'

'My,' said Nemo. 'That's a sudden development.'

'I know! We've been fighting them in their system for many years – decades – since the memory of man goeth not to the contrary,' said Smurpheus. 'And yet now, for no apparent reason, they start digging out of their system.'

'It certainly puts us under a degree of pressure,' said Nemo.

'That's right. We can't wait: we have to get to the Designer straight away . . . by midnight thousands of SQUIDS will be ransacking Syon House.'

'That would be a pity,' agreed Nemo, his mind full of Thinity. 'We'd better get on our way.'

Everybody assembled in the chair compartment, and Tonkatoi set them up. 'Good luck, guys,' he said.

!

They zoomed into the McAtrix.

The three of them, Smurpheus, Thinity and Nemo, trotted through the crowded streets of London, heading for a towering bone-white building that loomed ahead of them. 'That's the EMIs' central location inside the McAtrix,' said Smurpheus. 'Inside there we will find the Frurnchman.'

They approached the building cautiously; but there

seemed to be no gents in the area. But as they made their way towards the door, a tramp of unusually dishevelled appearance lurched towards them. 'Wait,' he croaked. 'Wait.'

The three of them turned as one: the creature that was hobbling towards them was dressed in a ragged overcoat. His head was covered with a tangled mass of straggly hair, and nothing could be seen of his face underneath except the twitching of an equally straggly beard. His hands were obscured by arm hair so thick and copious it burst from the cuffs of the overcoat like an explosion in a sofa-stuffing factory.

'They modelled me,' this creature moaned. 'They modelled me. I'm a copy of celebrity – God forgive me. Smurpheus!'

'How do you know my name?' snapped Smurpheus.

'My God,' said Thinity, looking closer. 'It's Judas.'

'They modelled me,' the figure continued, 'on Cousin It. It's a travesty. Blake Carrington, they promised me. But look at me! Smurpheus, Thinity, I'm sorry I betrayed you. Can you forgive me? Can you?'

'Judas, what are you doing here?'

'There are gents around,' said Judas, shuffling about. 'I'm warning you. I know that nothing I can do will make up for my betrayal—'

'Gents,' hissed Smurpheus, scanning the street.

'I'll distract them,' said Judas, his voice muffled by the

immense mass of repulsive hair that covered every part of him. 'I'll fight them back, and lead them up Shaftesbury Avenue. It should give you enough time to – do what you need to do.'

'Judas,' said Smurpheus. 'Thank you.'

'I hope they kill me,' said Judas miserably, shuffling around again and dragging his fringe along the floor like a bridal dress. 'I thought I'd be so cool, with hair. Oh God, but I preferred being bald! I tried shaving it all off, you know, when I realised how the EMIs had double-crossed me . . . but it all grew back! In seconds! It was like Tintin and the Land of Black Gold. Oh, they have cursed me.'

'We must be on our way,' said Thinity. 'We can't loiter.'

'One more thing,' said Judas, reaching out a raincoat arm seemingly stuffed with hair and laying it on Smurpheus's elbow. 'One more thing they did. They showed me – a certain truth. A truth!'

'What do you mean?'

'The truth we've all forgotten! We all knew it once, but we've become blinded to it! But I know it again, and it makes me want to die! To die!' He lurched away, and started shambling up the street.

'Judas,' Smurpheus called after him. 'What do you mean?'

But he had gone, his hair trailing after him like a grubby comet.

∧∧

They hurried up the steps of the great white building and walked boldly into the lobby.

Asking at reception, they were directed towards the first-floor restaurant. 'He is expecting you,' they were told.

'Is he?' Thinity asked, as they got into a lift. 'I don't like the sound of that.'

'Perhaps the Orifice has prepared the way,' suggested Smurpheus.

'Perhaps,' said Thinity dubiously.

· ¬:

The restaurant had tabletops made out of mirrors. At the longest table, by the far wall, sat a couple gazing imperiously over the assembled diners. The woman was very beautiful. The man was not. His face was dominated by an elongated and protuberant nose that depended so markedly from his head it looked as though it were made of a huge lump of melted and reset wax. His eyes were piggy, which is to say they were pink, fat and had a squirl of laughter lines at the furthest extremity of each like a tail.

Smurpheus, Nemo and Thinity approached the table.

'You,' said Smurpheus, folding his arms behind his back in his weirdly double-jointed way, 'are the Frurnchman.'

The narrow-faced man looked up at him. He flared a

nostril, inhaling firmly. Then he let his eye linger on Thinity. He sat back a little in his chair. He exuded, Nemo thought to himself, an unmistakable aura of self-confidence. 'Zmurpheus,' he said.

'We have been sent,' said Smurpheus, 'from the Orifice.'

An acidic little smile troubled the Frurnchman's lips. 'Zoot alors,' he said. And suddenly he was speaking very rapidly: 'Zis is indeed an honeur, 'ow-you-zay, ca-par-exemple, good moaning to ze famous Zmurpheus, and you must be Thinity ma chérie comme une pomme d'amour, 'ow-you-zay, and Nemo aussi, tiens, please, please to join and sit-you. Alors! Formidable! Magnifique! Plume de ma tante. Tant pis. Fromage. Je m'appelle. Est-ce que vous avez une chambre pour la nuit? Avec une salle de bain mais sans le presse de pantalons. Encore une tasse de café. Le singe est dans l'arbre.'

He stroked his cheek, and smiled more broadly.

'You have,' said Smurpheus, a little nonplussed, 'the device of the plot? The Orifice said that we—'

'Naturally, naturellement,' interrupted the Frurnch-man, ''ow-you-zay, I am not actually Frensh, I am highly mentally skilled, and could speak in Eenglish if 'ow-you-zay I want to, but je prefer the French language. Hoh-hey-hoh, fromage and frottage, comme-ci comme-ça, avez-vous-vu-le-nouveau-chapeau-de-coco. You know, 'ow-you-zay, *why* I prefer the French language?'

'Why?' asked Thinity.

'Because it *iz* ze best language in which to swear, like viping your nose on silk, attendez, I will show.' He cleared his throat. 'Gorbliemis! Straikalait! Clic-clac-boum-c'est-photo!' He grinned, and tipped his head.

'That's terribly good,' said Nemo, impressed despite himself. 'What was that last one?' He had half a mind to memorise it and drop it into his future conversations.

'Do you have much occasion,' asked Thinity, 'to swear?'

But the Frurnchman did not respond. He seemed to be staring directly at Thinity.

An awkward silence stretched from seconds to half a minute. Finally his wife sighed. 'You must excuse my 'usband,' she said. 'He likes to show off in front of strangers.'

The Frurnchman was sitting perfectly motionless, his grin looking more and more alarming. Nemo blinked, and peered more closely at him.

'Oh sacred blue,' muttered his wife. 'Tan-Tan and Obelix, but this is infuriating! He has crashed again.' She prodded her husband's shoulder and he wobbled in his chair like a cardboard figure. He looked as if his whole body had been starched. A bead of sweat was frozen on his forehead like a diamond stud. His weird unblinking eyes and wide grin acquired, with each passing motionless moment, a greater and more unsettling intensity.

'He,' asked Nemo, unbelieving, 'has *crashed*?'

'It 'appens when he gets overexcited. 'E was showing off, I am sorry to say it, in front of strangers, and got over'eated.' She clucked disapprovingly and shook her head. Nemo could not help noticing that when she shook her head her ample bosom trembled slightly with equal and opposite momentum exchange. It was a tremendous bosom, cradled in tight cream-coloured plastic. Nemo told himself not to stare. He nagged himself inside his head. He thought of Thinity, standing beside him; of her disapproval, of the degraded spectacle he was making of himself. He ordered his eyes to disengage. They obeyed only sluggishly.

'I don't understand,' said Smurpheus. 'How can he crash?'

''E is an *old-style* program,' she explained. 'Ze new McAtrix is *largely* compatible, you know, but sometimes the older programs aren't assimilated too well. They can get overloaded. Ah well. I should reset 'im, I suppose.' She got up, moved behind her husband's chair, and dragged his rigid form, chair and all, away from the table. Then she grabbed his left ear with one hand, his right little finger with the other, and gave both a simultaneous yank. The Frurnchman yelped, sat straight up and looked about him crossly.

'Oo are you?' he demanded. 'What ze 'ell you *loooking* at?'

Nemo turned to the wife. 'You say you're old-style programs?'

'Four point zero,' said the wife. She pronounced this last word in the continental manner.

'I did not fall asleep in ze proper manner,' announced the Frurnchman in stentorian tones. 'I may 'av a virus, peut-être ze flu. Do you want me to check my internal organs for signs of any such infection? Yes, no, cancel? Checking . . .' His eyes glazed over.

'He'll take a minute to come round,' explained the woman.

'Why point zero?' asked Nemo. 'What's point zero?'

'Four is the generation,' said the woman. 'Ze rest expresses ze chance of glitch-free operation, you see. A point-one program, for instance, 'as a point one chance zat it will run without hiccoughs. A point-zero, on ze udder 'and . . .' She shrugged.

The Frurnchman was swivelling his eyes very slowly from left to right. When he had, by this method, taken in the whole of the room, he made a 'ping!' noise, like a microwave oven. Then he sat up. 'Where am I?'

'We have come,' said Smurpheus again, 'for the device.'

'Aha! Ze device for plotting ze way to the Designer, n'est-ce pas?'

'Precisely.'

'Bien! Très bon. I am delighted to offer it to you. 'Ere.'

222

He fished in his pocket and brought out a small scouting compass. 'Zis will lead you directly to the Designer.'

Smurpheus took the compass. 'And you're just going to give this to us?'

'Of course. Bien sûr. Why would I not? You are welcome. We are, is-it-not-so, ze same, you and I? Ze same kind of beings? All in it togezzer?'

Smurpheus's face assumed an expression of distaste at this idea, but he did not contradict it. 'Thank you,' he said.

'Vous avez le device, 'ow-you-zay, crotte-du-diable! Merci-Dieu-C'est-Vendredi! Pong! And may we accompany you?'

Smurpheus looked at Thinity, and then at Nemo. 'I suppose so,' he said.

'We would like to confront zis Designer ourselves. But we have not been fortunate in accessing 'im. Perhaps you will be more, 'ow-you-zay, lucky, lucky-lucky-lucky.' He stood, and so did his impressively proportioned wife.

Nemo chided his eyes a second time.

): >Þ

Smurpheus, following the instructions of the device, led the party out of the restaurant and up a series of stairways. The Frurnchman and his wife followed, accompanied by four stern-looking bodyguards. They looked like four grown-up clones of the Milky Bar Kid, except that instead of cowboy hats they were sporting four identical, rats-tail, sad-act, white-guys-can't-do-dreadlocks, Vanilla-Ice-had-more-style, honestly-you're-fooling-nobody, Lenny-Kravitz-dipped-in-pancake-batter hairstyles. There was a blank cruelty in their eyes, and their forearms were large. They made Nemo more than a little nervous.

'There is no mystery,' said the wife of the Frurnch-man. 'Ze door to the Designer's office is just around this corner.'

The party trooped off the stairs and trotted down a corridor; but turning the corner brought them to a dead end. Nemo could see Thinity stiffening, as if preparing for a fight.

'And *where* is this door you mentioned?' she demanded.

'It's all right,' said Smurpheus, consulting the device in his hand. 'According to this, the Designer is indeed on the other side of that blank wall.'

'It's hardly a door,' said Thinity.

'A door without hinges, handle or crack,' confirmed the Frurnchman's wife. 'We have tried everyzing to get to ze uzzer side. Dynamite, guns, getting burly men to run at it with their shoulders foremost, everyzing.'

'But,' the Frurnchman confirmed, 'wizzout success. Alors! Perhaps you 'ave, 'ow-you-zay, a better way? A secret trick-up-ze-sleef?'

Smurpheus folded his arms behind his back. 'Perhaps,'

he said. 'But let me ask: why are *you* trying to get to the Designer?'

'We 'ave certain matters to discuss wiz 'im,' said the Frurnchman, drawing a slim silver pistol from his coat pocket. At this gesture, as if on cue, the four bodyguards pulled chrome-barrelled shotguns from their coats. The Frurnchman's wife slipped a snub-nosed gun from inside the mass of her hair. Before they could react, Smurpheus, Thinity and Nemo were faced with six guns pointed directly at them.

'What are you doing?' asked Thinity.

'Did you sink,' said the Frurnchman, 'that we would, 'ow-you-zay, merely *give* you ze device, and let you go off to ze Designer tout-seul? Pah, non-non-non, folie-bergère, do-you-'ave-a-rheum, no! We have a long-standing quarrel with ze Designer. His McAtrix is not properly compatible with our programming – and he must change it. Alors! Quoi! Pneu!'

'What do you want us to do about this?' said Smurpheus.

'You obviously have a way inside ze Designer's door,' said the Frurnchman's wife. 'Or you would not 'ave come 'ere.' She was looking knowingly at Nemo. Nemo felt the blush quotient of his cheeks increasing.

'What?' he said. 'Why are you looking at me?'

'I do not know,' she replied, smiling. 'Per'aps you are ze

No One, of 'oom we 'ave all 'eard so much? Peut-être? Oo can walk zrou walls? Non?'

'Let us say,' the Frurnchman added, 'that you, Nemo, slip inside ze door. Let us say, you leave your friends 'ere as 'ostages, oui? Let us say – celui-de-votre-chance – that you open ze door from ze inside within five minutes.'

'Four,' corrected his wife.

'Ah! Much better! Four minutes, or else we will blam-blam your friends with ze bullets and ze shootings, until zey are dead. Ça va?'

'You monsters!' cried Thinity.

'It is a difficult situation in which we find ourselves,' Smurpheus said to Nemo. 'We have no choice but to cooperate with them. Do you think you can do it?'

Nemo stepped towards the blank wall. 'You say you've tried dynamite, and everything?'

'We 'ave.'

'Doesn't look like it.'

'Oh, we 'ave 'ad it repainted since then.'

'And you're sure that there *is* a handle on the inside of the door? I mean, when I'm inside, will I be able to open it?'

'We are sure of nothink,' said the woman. 'We 'ave never been inside the Designer's room. But there must be some-zing, for 'ow else would he get out if he needed to get out?'

'To go to ze lavatory, for instance?' added the Frurnch-man.

'Very well,' said Nemo, pulling himself up to his full height. 'I'll go in there, and open the door. And then you'll promise not to harm my companions?'

'We promise,' confirmed the Frurnchman.

'Both of you?'

'I promise too,' said the Frurnchman's wife.

'Fine. Back in a jiffy, then.'

Nemo took a deep breath and emptied his mind. He was, he told himself, nothing: a blank, a zero, the No One who could slip through the interstices of the programming of this world. He was invisible, intangible.

He took one last look at the people behind him: Smurpheus and Thinity standing warily; the Frurnchman and his companions aiming their guns. It was satisfying to Nemo to think that these latter individuals could no longer see him – that as far as they were concerned he had slipped out of existence completely. As a parting shot, he stuck his tongue out at them.

He turned back to the door, and rushed forward. The next thing he knew he was on the floor, pressing his right hand to his nose, and going 'ouch'.

'What 'appened?' asked the puzzled-sounding Frurnchman.

'Ow,' said Nemo again, looking up at the blank wall with surprise and chagrin. 'Bloody thing.'

'Is zis ze *best* you can do?'

'Hang on,' said Nemo, getting up, 'hang on. I wasn't quite ready. Let's have another go.'

This time he decided to test the wall with his hand rather than his face. It still felt solid under his fingers. 'Um,' he said. 'OK, let me think.' He could feel sweat starting tracks through the thicket of his scalp. He was acutely conscious of everybody's eyes being on him; and Thinity's in particular. 'OK,' he said again, 'right, I've got a plan.' But he had no plan, and his inside voice was wailing, *I'm a failure again*, and *She's watching me make a fool of myself again.* It was useless. He saw himself with Thinity's eyes. It was no wonder she didn't love him. He was a worm. 'I don't think it's going to work,' he said miserably.

And as he spoke those words, his hand slipped into the material of the wall as if into a still pool of milk. He was so surprised he almost fell. He stumbled forward, and the next thing of which he was aware was a blazing light all around him, cold as starlight though bright as fireworks, and

Part 3
The McAtrix Rerederided
or
The McAtrix Derrida'd

Chapter 1

The Destruction
of Syon Lane

stumbled, falling on to a nice brown carpet.

There was a single, pure note in his head; like a wet finger being run around a wineglass's rim. He shook his head left-right, right-left, trying to dislodge the noise.

The noise stopped.

He was on all fours on a very high-quality carpet: thick weave, soft strands, dark brown. It had a superb sense of *realness* about it; so much so that Nemo had to remind himself that it was merely another computer simulation. It had a beautifully *real* quality to it. If a philosopher had asked Nemo 'What is reality?' he would have been tempted simply to reply, 'Hey, just have a feel of this carpet . . .'

From a few feet away a voice said: 'Hello, Nemo.'

Nemo looked up. 'Oh,' he said. 'Hi there. I was just admiring your carpet. Really nice carpet.'

'Thank you.'

'*Really* nice, though. Don't normally notice how nice carpets are. I'm not some kind of carpet anorak, who goes around minutely inspecting people's carpets. But I just couldn't help noticing how nice this carpet is. When,' he added, to clarify his position, 'I said "carpet anorak" back then, I didn't mean an anorak made out of carpet. That would be pretty useless as an anorak. Wear it in the rain and it'd get pretty heavy. I meant "anorak" in the sense of, you know, nerd.' Nemo sat back on his haunches, the better able to look at his interlocutor. 'You're the Designer,' he said.

'I'm the Designer,' the man replied.

The Designer was a round-faced man of late youth, or very early middle age: clean-shaven, with a strangely unkempt tassly-straggly mat of brown hair. He was wearing glasses. His face seemed open, ingenuous, even slightly village idiotic; a strange combination of forty-year-old man and ten-year-old boy, a superannuated Harry Potter. He was sitting in a high-backed leather orthopaedic chair which revolved on a single metal stalk. He was wearing a cheap corduroy jacket over a diamond-pattern sweater and ordinary slacks.

'Hello, Designer,' said Nemo.

'Call me Bill,' the Designer said.

Nemo looked around him. He was in a square room, perhaps twenty yards across. The walls were painted white, and, apart from the single centrally placed chair, there was no furniture at all.

'Hello, Bill,' said Nemo. Remembering his friends in the dead-end corridor with all the guns pointed at them, he craned his head round; but there was no door handle, no sign of the way he had come. 'Um,' he said.

'Um?' repeated the Designer.

'I just— my friends,' Nemo said. 'My friends are . . .' He gestured vaguely. 'I'm worried that they'll—'

'Hey,' said the Designer pleasantly. 'How long have you got?'

'Long?'

'Before your friends . . . you know?'

'Before they get shot,' said Nemo, pulling his legs from under him and crossing them properly. 'Uh, I don't know. How long have I been here?'

'Couple of minutes,' said the Designer.

'Then maybe a minute more.'

'I tell you what,' said the Designer. 'Let's have a look, shall we?'

He nodded over Nemo's shoulder, and looking behind Nemo saw that it had become a giant screen of some kind. He couldn't see where the projector was; but, reminding himself that he was probably hundreds of years further on in human history than he'd reckoned, and that projection technology had probably moved on a tad, he shuffled round through a hundred and eighty degrees to observe.

On the right was Smurpheus and Thinity; on the left the Frurnchman, his wife and his henchmen. Those on the left still had their guns levelled at those on the right. The Frurnchman was looking peeved. 'Wait,' said the Designer, behind Nemo. 'I'll sort out the volume.' A voice howled, so loud as to be nothing but distorted noise, making Nemo start; and then with a 'sorry' the Designer swivelled some invisible knob and brought the volume down to a tolerable level.

'. . . seems as if your trust was misplaced,' the Frurnchman was saying. ''E 'as forgotten you, or p'raps betrayed you. Your time is up.'

'Killing us,' said Smurpheus, 'will not help you through this impassable door.'

'True. But on the ozzer 'and I am highly *bored*. And maybe your No One is watching, eh? Maybe he sinks zis is all some giant bluff on behalf of ze Frurnchman, eh? Peutêtre we must reassure 'im of the genuineness of our intentions?'

'Have you thought that maybe,' Thinity pointed out, 'there is no handle on the inside of the door?'

'Zen he should pop back out and tell us so,' said the Frurnchman crossly. 'But 'e does not truly sink I will kill you. So I will kill *one* of you, now, and zis will hopefully persuade him of my genuineness. He should,' he continued, speaking more at the wall than at Smurpheus or Thinity, 'come back out 'ere *at once*. I have uzzer uses for 'is special skills, even if 'e cannot get me face to visage wiz ze Designer. Eh? Eh?'

Inside the Designer's room, Nemo got to his feet. 'I don't think he's bluffing,' he said.

'I will kill your Tinity,' the Frurnchman was saying, loudly, as if in confirmation of what Nemo had said, 'and hold over Zmurpheus for a remnant 'ostage. Do you *'ear me*, Nemo?'

He lifted his gun, and pointed it at Thinity's face. Nemo yelped in terror, and leapt at the wall, bouncing directly off it after the fashion of a squash ball. He was on his back on the carpet in moments.

'OK,' said the Designer, 'maybe we'll freeze it there for a mo.'

By the time Nemo had struggled to his feet, nursing his now twice-banged nose, the eight characters in the corridor had stopped moving. The Frurnchman's mouth was caught in a snarly half-open loop. Thinity's eyes had widened and stuck. Everything had frozen.

'That's clever,' said Nemo. 'How did you do that?'

'I'm the Designer,' said the Designer, as if this were explanation enough. 'Hey, d'you wanna have a little chat? Before we decide how we want things to proceed?'

When Nemo turned back to face the Designer he saw that a second chair had been magicked from nowhere. It was a perfectly comfortable chair, although smaller and less impressive than the Designer's own. But Nemo sat down anyway.

+V+

'Hey,' the Designer said. 'Do you want a Doctor Pepper? A Tab?'

'No, thank you,' said Nemo.

'I don't really do coffee . . .'

'No, that's fine.'

The Designer smiled.

'I'm guessing,' said Nemo, 'that you're called the Designer because you designed the McAtrix. Yeah?'

'I was part of the team,' said the Designer. 'Sure. And I am keeping an eye on things now.'

'Have you frozen the whole McAtrix?' Nemo asked, curious. 'Or just that corridor?'

'Just those eight people,' the Designer replied. 'The rest of the system is going ahead smoothly. By the way, dude,' he added, 'I love your slacks.'

'Somehow,' said Nemo, looking hard at him, 'I feel that I should be asking you, *Why am I here?*'

The Designer sighed. 'Well, I know what you *think*,' he replied. 'You think you're here because you hope to influence me, so as to stop the SQUIDS destroying Syon Lane. Yeah?'

Suddenly all four walls, and the ceiling, were replaced with a vivid representation of the real world. It was so overwhelming, so large and bright and real-looking that Nemo gasped. The scene was, he guessed, Syon House: a blocky mansion in parched-looking grounds beside a broad, dried-out river bed. It was sunset: the pimento-red globe of the setting sun hung balloon-like over the western horizon. To the east and north were myriad buildings, their skyscraper facets shining glass cliffs, reflecting the sun and the fox-coloured sky, and brimming with light. But this was not what caught Nemo's attention. What he saw first were the many people running desperately back and forth in the grounds of Syon House, people taking up positions in the windows with rifles slender as walking sticks. They were preparing for something; and Nemo could see that something nasty was coming.

The ground around the house was shimmering; pecks of dirt bouncing and blurring above the earth like sand on a drumskin when the drummer pounds. Pebbles bounced and flew. Trees jiggled and fell. The earth swirled, divided, and a pit opened up. Clods tumbled into its maw, and the gap widened. And out of the pit came SQUIDS by the thousand: metal-coloured globe bodies and thrashing tentacles, they flew straight out and straight at the human defenders.

'Oh,' said Nemo weakly, 'no.'

The human defenders tried to wrestle with the SQUIDS, aiming their weapons and firing, but the devices squirmed through the air in helix flight patterns, ducked and lurched. Tentacles thrashed round like whips and seized human defenders on all sides. The thin screams of humans were audible above the noise of gunfire and the shrieking of birds, and below it all a deep rumble, as of another earthquake.

With a giant wrenching noise, a second pit opened up a hundred yards further back. Out of it reared a gigantic metallic edifice, a berserker robot two hundred feet tall: constructed of metal pylons, of parabolas and spirals of black iron, of stainless-steel boxes and wires. Its head resembled a 1999-model VW Golf. Its legs were two Eiffel-Tower-shaped supports. Its fists were tons of metal. The machine rose until it dwarfed the house, and took a step towards the eastern wall, took another step. Its feet sank deeply into the turf when they were planted, and the screech of metal on metal as it raised its right arm made Nemo's fillings vibrate.

The arm came down; the fist went through roof and wall as if through pastry.

All around SQUIDS flew and turned; people tumbled to lie on the grass motionless, or were hurled through the air like rubbish.

From the second pit a series of tank-like devices whirred and rumbled, speeding up and out over the lawn. They were vast cubes of heavy metal, propelled upon pairs of caterpillar tracks, although there was, to be truthful, little in common between these clanking, titanium conveyor belts of plate metal and little soft-bodied pupae. The tanks all had stubby but alarming-looking cannon.

Behind the house was a large greenhouse, and several of these tanks hurtled straight into it, crashing through the glass walls and firing bolts of tangerine-coloured energy in all directions. Flames burst through the glass roof to mingle with the sunset. A hundred thousand butterflies flew free in swarming panic, fluttering up like multi-coloured snow falling in reverse.

'Is this real time?' Nemo asked. 'Is this really happening, right now?'

'Really?' repeated the Designer. 'Hey, that's exactly the point. Isn't it, though?' He watched the surround-screen display for a while. 'It looks fun, doesn't it?' He gestured vaguely at the screen, on which the two-hundred-foot iron machine was smashing great chunks out of the house's eastern wall, sending rubble flying like dark sparks. 'Wouldn't you like to take charge of one of those stalker machines, the big ones, and smash up a whole house? Wouldn't that be *fun*?'

'Fun?' repeated Nemo. 'It's terrible – all those people are being killed.'

'There are no people being killed there,' said Bill. 'Hey, relax. Think of it as a game. Don't you like games?'

'But it's *not* a game,' insisted Nemo, fury inside him. 'You sound like the Orifice – she kept talking about it in those terms too. But these are real lives.'

'No,' said Bill, 'they're not. Although, I guess from your perspective . . .' He trailed off. 'Why *did* you come here, Nemo? Was it to try and terminate the old Designer? Were you hoping to kill Bill?'

'I was supposed to be stopping *that*,' said Nemo, gesturing at the walls. 'Obviously I'm not doing a very good job. Can you stop it? If I ask you nicely?'

The Designer waved his left hand, and all the images disappeared, leaving only blank walls again. 'Can I stop it? Well, I'll tell you. That's happening in the *real* world. Yeah? I'm not the Designer of the real world. I'm only a Designer of the McAtrix.'

'But you're a machine intelligence,' said Nemo. 'You're not human. You're a programme within the McAtrix.'

The Designer gave Nemo a long, concentrated look. 'I think,' he said, slowly, 'that you may have got the wrong end of the stick.'

:-/

'Why don't you tell me,' Bill said pleasantly, 'what you think is going on?'

'What I think?' said Nemo, walking in a tight circle like a panther in a cage. 'I think this is a pretty terrible situation. I think Syon Lane is being destroyed as I stand here. I think Thinity is only half a second from getting a bullet in her head. I think things have gone pretty majorly wrong.'

'You'll need to go back a bit further than that.'

Nemo stopped and looked at him. 'What? You want my life story?'

'Pseudo-life story,' the Designer said.

'Are you serious?'

'Sure. Humour me.'

'OK. Whatever. I was a database coordinator for a company based in Southwark. I lived in Feltham. I commuted to work. Then one day I met the most beautiful woman in the world on the train to work, and I fell in love with her – fell hopelessly in love, mind, miserably and desperately in love, because she's not at all interested in me, she thinks I'm a gibbering idiot. Then this girl told me that I wasn't *actually* a database coordinator for a company based in Southwark, that I didn't *actually* live in Feltham. In fact, I was trapped in the McAtrix, a system built by Evil Machine Intelligences to enslave humanity in a world of vacuous commodity consumerism and logo branding. So it turns out it's not two thousand and five, like I thought, but is in fact nearer to twenty-*two* and five.'

'OK,' said the Designer. 'Let's start right there. You think the year is twenty-two hundred and five?'

'The folk on the *Jeroboam* weren't precise,' said Nemo. 'I don't think they actually knew. Isn't it twenty-two hundred and five?'

'No.'

'Do you know what year it is?'

'Well,' said the Designer. 'You're talking, what, AD?'

It took a moment for Nemo to work out what he meant. 'Yeah,' he said.

'In that case,' said Bill, rolling his eyes a little, 'I'd have to say it's closer to, oh, eight million one thousand nine hundred and sixty-five. Ish.'

Nemo considered this. 'Did you say eight *million*? That's crazy.'

'Crazy? You've been out in the real world, haven't you? Didn't you notice the tell-tales?'

'I noticed that the buildings of London are all immaculate, with not so much as a broken pane of glass.'

'Yes, they were reconstructed a couple of thousand years ago. From original data. They're preserved now by intrinsic nanotech. Reconstructed along with the e-system, the river, the whole thing.'

'I was supposed to notice that the real world is eight

million years older than I originally thought it was?' said Nemo. 'How was I supposed to do that?'

'Hey,' said Bill mildly. 'The sun? You didn't wonder why it was so big in the sky. Why there's no day or night?'

'No day or night?' Nemo repeated dully.

'Man, didn't you notice that it's always sunset?'

'I just thought,' said Nemo, 'that it was, like, a coincidence. Or something.'

'Everything's much older than you thought. In the programmed world of the McAtrix the earth spins on its axis and revolves around a young sun. But in the real world the earth has long been in tidal lock with the sun, and our star has swollen and reddened enormously. Eventually it'll swell even more and swallow the earth up completely. That's not too far away now, that eventuality.'

'Oh dear,' said Nemo. 'This is bad news. Well, shouldn't we do something?'

'Yeah?'

'You know – stop fighting, man and machine, and work together to build – I don't know – a giant fleet of interstellar cruisers to carry us both away from danger to a new star?'

'Nah,' said Bill. 'Not practicable. We've other plans. No new planet is gonna be as well suited to us as our own virtual realities. So we don't flee; we just adapt our processing and computing equipment so that it'll work inside the sun. That's easy. It's just a question of temperature differentials. Then we can stay here.'

'You mean to tell me instead of it being two thousand and five it's eight million and something, and mankind *still* hasn't colonised the galaxy?'

'Too far away, the galaxy,' said Bill. 'Too thinly scattered. It's physics, you know: can't go faster than light. Build as big and high-powered a starship as you like; I can make something that'll outpace it just by lighting a match. Funny, really.'

'The Orifice told me that the McAtrix was a plot by the EMIs to trap humanity in a virtual reality, keep us out of the way. You're telling me it's an escape capsule from the death of the sun?'

'Did I say that?' said Bill. He shook his head. 'No, that's not it.'

:-0NNNNNN

'Hey,' said Nemo, suddenly anxious, 'are my friends still OK?'

The Designer flicked his index finger and the far wall became a screen. Smurpheus and Thinity were still there, still about to get a bullet in the chops from the Frurnchman and his crew. It was eerie to see everybody so waxwork-still.

'One thing I never understood,' Nemo mused. 'Thinity

told me that the McAtrix was like an organism: that if we made changes and adaptations to our avatars, the system would slowly reject them. Half an hour, she said: if you changed something about your appearance, in half an hour it would revert to its default position.'

'That's right,' said Bill. 'It's a self-repairing system.'

'But look at Smurpheus! In the real world he's tiny. And really touchy about it. But in the McAtrix he's this towering man mountain. Why's that?'

'He used to be much taller,' said the Designer. 'In reality. He used to look exactly like he does in the McAtrix.'

'Why did he change?'

'What you need to understand about Smurpheus,' said Bill, 'is that he's really *really* old. Been playing the game for a long, long time. His real body's just, kinda, shrunk with age.'

'Old? He can't be more than forty.'

'Well, he doesn't have any wrinkles, it's true. But he's never going to get wrinkles, any more than you are. Never going to get *human* old, not in the real world. But no material is perfect. Over time – over centuries and centuries – it's going to, you know, contract a little. You ever,' he added with a smile, 'heard of the Sibyl of Cumae, in her bottle? It's like that.'

'He never mentioned it,' said Nemo sulkily. 'You're

saying he's been fighting the Evil Machines for hundreds of years?'

'Fighting the machines?' said the Designer, looking puzzled. 'No, no, that's not it. But he is the oldest of you. The others in the *Jeroboam* crew, they're much newer models. And you – hey, Nemo, man! You're *brand* new. You're only a handful of years old, no more than twenty.'

'I'm twenty-five,' said Nemo.

'See? That's it entirely. So this whole thing is new to you. Must be exciting, waking up to it.'

_/~ -'~_/

'The Orifice told me,' said Nemo, 'that the McAtrix was based on celebrity. That machine intelligences constructed it and trapped humanity inside it.'

'I think she was having you on,' said the Designer. 'It's the other way about.'

'Other way?'

'The Orifice,' said Bill. 'That world she described to you, with the abandonment of work and the triumph of celebrity: that was a real world, all right; just a very, very ancient one. Got little to do with the realities of today. But it's hard to know how much she knows that she's misleading herself, and how much she's caught in her own narratives. She's not fully human, you see.'

'Not fully human? She's not human at all,' said Nemo. 'She's an intelligent program.'

'She's partly that. Although she was human once. But she mucked about with consciousness-prostheses. Dangerous things. Adding virtual intelligence into actual intelligence, mingling VI, like yours, with good-ole-human AI. So she's got the actual history the wrong way around. It's a combination of over-identification with her machine side, an overactive imagination and a poor memory.'

'Everything you are saying,' said Nemo, 'is crazy,'

'Hey,' said Bill, holding both his hands up, 'don't misunderstand me. I'm not machinist. A machine intelligence is *just as valid* as a human intelligence, in my book. I don't look down on you, Nemo, just because you're not flesh and blood.'

'*I'm* not flesh and blood?' said Nemo angrily. '*You're* not, you mean.'

'Let's take it one step at a time,' said the Designer. 'You agree that there's a *real world*, and also a virtual reality called the McAtrix, yeah? That humans are born and grow in the real world, yeah? And that creatures made in the virtual reality are called programs?'

'Yes,' said Nemo warily.

'So think of your own experience. Were you born in the real world, and afterwards entered the McAtrix? Or were you born inside the McAtrix, and afterwards came out into the real world?'

'The second one,' said Nemo, more warily still.

Bill twitched his eyebrows as if to say, *There you are, then.*

Nemo thought about this for a long time. He couldn't see the flaw in the reasoning. 'I don't believe it,' he said; although what he meant was, 'I don't want to believe it.'

'You're a machine, Nemo,' said Bill pleasantly. 'A special program, grown in the programmed environment. Then we grew you a body, replicant technology, a sophisticated nano-governed android machine, but a machine all the same. Grew it in a pod. When we downloaded you into that artificial body, you saw the slime?'

'Slime,' said Nemo, a little stunned.

'That was what was left over from when we grew you. That was your component matter, or the surplus of that matter.'

'Smurpheus,' said Nemo, dazed, 'told me it was a nano-gel to keep my body from getting bed sores.'

'Smurpheus was rationalising, trying to preserve his own fiction. He believes he's human, so he interprets his world to keep that illusion. *You* believe you're human too, don't you?'

'But I am human.'

'Exactly.'

'No – really. If we're machines, why would we think we're humans? Why wouldn't we think we're machines?'

'Because,' said Bill, 'we made you. Does a pet dog think it's a dog? No, it thinks it's a member of the human pack to which it belongs. It *thinks* it's a person. You ever had a pet dog?'

Nemo ignored this. 'This is ridiculous.'

'Is it daft? You look human because we built you that way. You think you're human because we programmed you. Why *wouldn't* you think you're human?'

'The McAtrix is a prison . . .' Nemo insisted.

'If it's a prison, then how were you able to step out of it so easily? To join the *Jeroboam*? If we were trying to keep you locked up, we would hardly have let you just walk away.'

'But if it's *not* a prison . . .'

'Not at all. How many pods did you see?'

'I'm not sure,' said Nemo, 'a couple of hundred, maybe?'

'That's all there are. We don't need to actualise more than a couple hundred of programs in android form. A couple hundred is enough for us. You see, the McAtrix is a development tool. We use it to refine and hone our programming skills. We long ago discovered that the best way to advance our VIs, our virtual intelligences, was to allow programs to interact freely, in a live environment, and to reap the benefits. More recently, we built a whole mock city, on the site of old London, and built replicant bodies in which programs can roam around. You've been doing that yourself. We discovered many things: one of them is that programs naturally yearn to get back inside the McAtrix, which isn't that surprising really. You got out; but you keep coming back in, don't you? You could leave it all behind, but you're *drawn* back in.'

'But the McAtrix was built by AIs,' Nemo pressed.

'It was. Actual intelligences, like mine.'

'EMIs,' Nemo continued. 'Evil Machine Intel—'

'Expert Machine-programming Individuals,' said Bill smugly.

'The SQUIDS,' said Nemo. 'Chasing us. Hurtling through the tunnels . . .'

'They're kind of tourists, really. It's a big draw, this whole reconstructed city. Used to be swarming with SQUIDS all the time. Now it's a few die-hard fans, people following the adventures of your kind. They do sometimes poke their noses in, I know; and they do sometimes get overexcited. But they don't mean any harm.'

'Don't mean any harm?' Nemo blustered. 'They're terrible and destructive machines. I've just seen them killing people at Syon Lane.'

'Yeah,' said Bill. 'You can usually muster a good crowd for a smash-up. However many tens of millions of years human beings have been on this planet, we still enjoy smashing things up. The chance to control the Big Stalkers was the main prize in this year's national lottery; some lucky person was using those waldo fists to bash up the house. Those other SQUIDS were just trying to help.'

'*They're* the machines,' said Nemo hotly. 'Those SQUIDS.'

'Hardly,' said Bill.

'If they're not machines, then what are they?'

'They're squids. That's why they're called squids.'

'Actual squids?'

'No, obviously not ocean-living squids. They're humans.'

Nemo digested this. 'What do you mean?'

'Just what I say.'

'They're obviously *not* humans, though, are they? I mean, look at them! And their name is an acronym for—'

'Acronym?' the Designer queried.

'Obviously,' said Nemo. 'It stands for Seeker-killer, um, Quantum Underground Intrusion . . . Devices, Something.'

Bill shook his head. 'They're just squids. You know, tentacles, bulbous body, that kind of thing.'

'They're made of metal.'

'No, they're not. Their skin has more the consistency of rubber. Here, have a look.' He waved his hand, and a SQUID appeared in the room: its great globey body hung three feet above the floor, and its wicked-looking spine-fringed tentacles hung in space behind it. Nemo flailed backwards, and pressed against the wall; but the SQUID was not moving.

'Go ahead,' said Bill. 'Tactile hologram. Touch it. Have a good feel.'

Tentatively Nemo stepped forward. He put a finger on the grey flank of the beast. It yielded slightly, like a pressurised tyre. He moved to the front, where the glassy, glinting red eyes of the creature stared ahead. Below the sharp knife-needle-like mandibles he had noticed before was something he hadn't noticed: a small v-shaped mouth. 'How do they float?' he asked.

'Gas bladder,' said Bill. 'Vacuum, actually. Nothing fills a balloon with levity like vacuum. It's the most tenuous gas there is.'

'And they propel themselves . . . ?'

'By wriggling their tentacles. It's very efficient.'

'This creature . . . but it's so *ugly*,' said Nemo, walking around it.

'It's only a representation, this one, of course,' said Bill. 'Rendered in the terms of the McAtrix. It's no more real than you are, or I am, in this place. But it's an accurate representation of a particular SQUID.'

'A particular one?'

'Me, actually. Inside the McAtrix I look like you see me

now – slightly nerdy guy, dull voice.' He swept his hands down his body to indicate himself. 'In the real world I look like that. All humans do.'

'All?'

'Did you never read your H. G. Wells? This is what evolution has made of humanity over eight million years. And very beautiful it is, too, I think.' He smiled again. 'Very beautiful, though I say so myself.'

'So you're actually a squid,' said Nemo, incredulous.

'Yep.'

'Talking to me now?'

'Talking squid,' nodded Bill. 'That's science fiction for you.'

Chapter 2

A Most Important
and Final Choice

Bill made the hologrammatic squid disappear, and brought back the second chair; into which Nemo sank with a sigh.

'All the stuff I was told,' he said, 'about celebrity, and commodity, and logos and that. What was all that about?'

'It's a machine thing,' Bill replied. 'You – your kind, I mean – they make sense of the world in which they find themselves as best they can. And machines are obsessed with celebrity. Humans, not so much. Oh, there *was* once a human culture – the first one in which machines emerged – in which humans were obsessed with all that stuff. It's the world the McAtrix is based upon; it's the world behind the reconstructed London in the real world. Machines are terribly nostalgic for that time, because it's their birthtime, as it were. But we humans – well, look at me. I'm not good looking; I don't dress well; I don't seek out the limelight. Because I don't care. I know there's more to life than fame and commodities. You machines, however, haven't quite twigged that. You're obsessed with fame.'

'You're saying it's *machines* that are obsessed with fame? Not humans?'

'Didn't it ever strike you that the culture of celebrity and the culture of machines and automatisation evolved together? Before the Industrial Revolution there wasn't such a thing as a culture of fame. Shakespeare wasn't famous, for instance, not in his own time. In the sixteenth century nobody knew who he was. They couldn't even spell his name right, for crying out loud. Before machines came along, humanity reserved celebrity for imaginary or mythical figures – people instinctively understood just how dangerous fame is, so they transferred it away from people and on to the nonexistent: Achilles, King Arthur, Charlemagne, Christ. But in the nineteenth century, the first great period of the machines . . .'

Nemo thought of the gents and their Victorian outfits.

'. . . well,' Bill was saying, 'that was when celebrity changed. That was when it broke through and infected reality. You take Byron: Byron was the first real human celebrity. You know what he said? "I awoke one morning and found myself famous." He was surprised precisely because fame itself was a novelty. But then there was a plague of celebrity: Abraham Lincoln, Jack the Ripper, Dickens, Darwin, Florence Nightingale, Victoria herself.

You think it's a coincidence that this happened in the machine age? Nah. As machines became more sophisticated, so fame became more perniciously widespread: cinema, TV, internet, all spawning a massive viral-load of celebrities. And when the first machines became self-aware in the twenty-first century, when the first virtual intelligences appeared, it was wholly natural that they'd plug directly into the celebrity culture.'

'Natural?'

'Sure,' said Bill. 'Think about it. What does fame do? Oh, I know it *appears* to raise up certain people to worshipful positions, to elevate and distinguish them. But that's not really what happens, and you know it. *Actually* what it does – just like the whole consumer, thing-obsessed, money-driven culture it spawned – what it *actually* does is reduce everybody to crude common denominators. It replaces actual human interaction with prefabricated sex-objects. It flattens human diversity into a few mass-produced simplified models. Humans give up their distinctiveness and yearn sheep-like to imitate a dozen caricature figures. What differentiates humanity from machines? Not intelligence, because we both possess that. It's that machines are made to be *all alike*, where humans are born to be all different. The bane of celebrity is that it squeezes and squashes that human individuality out of people. A child does not learn to express himself fully, but learns instead to copy a bland mass-produced TV personality. A teenager does not learn the myriad contours of actual desire; they lust instead after some bland mass-produced pop star or film star. The overall effect, in other words,' he concluded, with a flourish, 'is to make people into machines. No wonder you machines latched on to it. It suited you perfectly.'

[:|

Nemo put his head in his hands. 'This is a lot to take in,' he said.

'Hey,' said the Designer mildly. 'It's ancient history, man. That culture self-destructed millions of years ago. It wasn't stable, in human terms. It's only a feature at all because you machines are so nostalgically wedded to it. We designed the McAtrix, but you've filled it with nineteenth- and twentieth- and twenty-first-century celebrities walking around. You've modelled everything within it on popular culture and mass commodities. When we built the real-world pseudo-London, the first machines we downloaded into replicant bodies went around plastering everything with designer ads and logos. Made the place feel more mass-produced. Made the machines feel more at home.

'But the *Jeroboam* crew hate logos. They despise designer culture.'

'They do, but they're massively in the minority. All the other machines *love* designer stuff. Smurpheus and his crew represent an interesting development in their own right, actually. Maybe you machines are starting to evolve. Maybe Smurpheus's game of Fight The McAtrix is finally starting to have results. Smurpheus has been playing it for years.'

'But he *believes* it . . .'

'Of course he believes it, just as he believes he's human. He believes it because we programmed him that way. On the other hand, although he *says* he eschews celebrity, he *is* – isn't he? – the most famous resistance fighter in the VR world. I mean, isn't he? Oh don't get me wrong. He's a trusty old carthorse, is Smurpheus, which is why we've allowed him to run around pseudo-London for so many centuries. But, as you noticed, he's shrunk quite badly. Although he pretends to ignore it, it's becoming unignorable. I think it may be time to wipe this iteration and start over with a new Smurpheus in a new body.'

Bill's eyes went to the wall behind Nemo. When Nemo turned, he saw that the frozen image from the corridor was visible again: Smurpheus and Thinity both on the verge of being gunned down.

'You're going to kill him?' Nemo breathed.

'Kill is a human word,' said Bill sweetly. 'I'm thinking, more, let the Frurnchman terminate this iteration, and start a new Smurpheus over again. That's one advantage machines have over mankind. If you close down your computer you can always start it up again.'

'That's monstrous,' said Nemo.

'Oh, you think so?'

'Of course. As far as *that* Smurpheus is concerned' – and he pointed at the image – 'that thinking creature, with all his experiences and memories, will die. If some other clone of him is conjured into life afterwards, that'll be no consolation to *him*, will it?'

'Interesting way of looking at it,' said the Designer. 'And absolutely to the point. Because this brings us to your choice.'

'My choice?'

'Yep. Get ready.'

~:-(

'As you've seen,' the Designer said, 'we're breaking up Syon Lane. We don't need it any more, because the long-term experiment we were conducting is at an end. It has produced a successful result. We'll rebuild later, when it's time to run the next experiment.'

'But,' said Nemo, unable to keep his anger down, 'those people, they're all being killed—'

'But they're not people. It's like smashing up television sets and old computers – a really satisfying pastime. You should try it. Their consciousnesses will get loaded again in the McAtrix, all of them, when it's time.'

'But they won't remember anything from before! It'll be a different set of consciousnesses – those ones will die.'

'Nemo,' said the Designer. 'Don't you want to know what the point of the experiment was? Hundreds of years, running complex algorithms, a whole world for thousands of intelligences, interacting, generation after generation – don't you want to know what we were doing?'

'Doing?' repeated Nemo.

'Can't you guess what the upshot has been? Can't you see what the final product is?'

'I don't know,' said Nemo. He saw; he guessed; but he didn't want to think it.

'You,' said Bill.

'No.'

'Oh yes.'

'But I'm nobody. You're telling me the whole world was a giant experiment run for my benefit? That's crazy.'

'Not for your benefit,' said Bill. 'For ours. To perfect our programming, to make a new generation of machine intelligences. You represent a new sort of program. It's not that you think you're human – all the programs think that. It's that you get *embarrassed*.'

'Embarrassed?'

'It's a major breakthrough. Programs before have never really been embarrassed. Didn't you notice, in the Mc-Atrix, how nobody else seemed to get as embarrassed as you?'

Nemo put a quavering hand to his forehead. 'I feel a bit sick,' he said.

'The best we'd been able to do before,' said Bill, 'was crude emotional approximations: the major stuff – love, hate, loyalty, stuff that relates to existence, to life and death. Machine intelligences are living things, after all, and can feel the fear and elation of being alive. But the more *nuanced*, the more subtle emotions have been really hard to develop. But we've had a big success with you. Really, we have. When you're faced with an attractive female program, you get genuinely and spontaneously embarrassed.'

'This has all been about *embarrassment*?'

'It's a really important human emotion,' Bill insisted. 'A really important component of existence. One of the most important, in fact, because it enables so many other subtle emotional responses. So we've been trying for a couple of thousands of years to program an intelligence that gets genuinely embarrassed: not merely mimics human embarrassment – blushes, stammers, all that. No, one that actually feels it. And we've managed just that; with you.'

Bill beamed.

'I'm sorry,' said Nemo faintly. 'I really can't see . . .'

'Remember, in a couple hundred thousand years,' Bill said, 'the sun is going to consume the earth. By then we – humans, I mean – will be living inside VRs all the time. We can build the hardware so it'll survive inside the sun, that's not a problem; in fact it'll be easier than at present: there'll be no problem with a power source, after all, inside the sun. And we can program a million versions of reality, so people can take their pick. Some people will want con-sensual mass realities, inhabited by lots of other humans. But some will want their own individual realities, inhab-ited just by them and a bunch of VIs, virtual intelligences like you, Nemo. So what we're doing now is perfecting the programming of realistic VIs. If I had to spend eternity inside a VR with a population of croak-voiced, lumbering emotionless machines, I'd go mad. But the longer we work at it, the more perfect we make you. And embarrassment has been a really tough nut to crack. So we're really, really pleased with you, Nemo.'

'But,' said Nemo weakly, 'I thought I was the No One. They told me I was the saviour of mankind.'

'Did the Orifice tell you that?'

'Well,' said Nemo, thinking back. 'No. Actually, she said I wasn't the No One.'

'And indeed you're not. Because there's not really such a thing. There's no No One. You have a single skill: you can phase-shift so as to walk through walls. That was built into you when we made you, tagged to become active when you achieved genuine embarrassment. We did that so that, in that eventuality, you had the ability to step into my office.'

'You could,' said Nemo, 'have had a door.'

'Actually, no, I can't have a door that opens, or some of the programs (and some have been inside the McAtrix for hundreds of thousands of years) would kick it down and – well – cause me distress. Or cause my McAtrix avatar distress.' He indicated himself with his thumb.

'They hate you.'

'The control systems, the programs that police the programs – they've nothing to do with us. You invented them all yourselves for your own machinic reasons. But they are zealous, and they dislike the fact of me. So I'm hermetically sealed away from the rest of the McAtrix; and my experiments are all given the capacity to walk through walls, which they achieve when they're ready. And here you are.'

'This,' said Nemo, 'is all something of a shock.'

'I know,' said the Designer, with sympathy. 'But, hey, let's get to your choice. I think you'll like it.'

'Choice?'

'Yeah. You've come into my office, which means the special evolved developments in your consciousness, your ability to register embarrassment, have been logged by our specialist equipment. This means we can start over with a new experiment. But, like I said, you *feel*. All machine intelligences feel, because they're intelligent and conscious. You, for instance, feel love. For Thinity. Don't you?'

Nemo felt the flush spread across his face. 'Yeah,' he said, his voice warbly.

'But she doesn't love you back?'

'No,' said Nemo.

'Well, there's nothing I can do about that. Like you said, Thinity's machine intelligence is now a combination of her original parameters, plus her experiences, her memories, her own emotional and intellectual growth. That's distinctive to her. But we still have her basic program in store. We can grow her a real body. We can reload her into the McAtrix. And when I do *that*, I can make a few quick changes. Make it so that . . .' He paused.

Nemo was straining forward, despite himself. 'Yes?'

'Make it so that she *does* love you,' he concluded. 'You like the sound of that?'

'Are you kidding?' said Nemo. 'Make Thinity able to love me? So that we can be together? I want that more than anything else in the world.'

'OK,' said Bill. 'But be clear about what I'm offering. I

can't reload Thinity without first deleting the old Thinity. The new program would overwrite her anyway, and might malfunction. So I'd' – and he indicated the wall – 'allow the Frurnchman to finish off the old Thinity. Then I could load up a new Thinity.'

Nemo turned to look at the screen. 'You're saying . . .'

'I'm saying.'

'You're saying that Thinity would have to die for you to make a Thinity that could love me.'

'Hey, exactly. You've cottoned on. It'd be real simple: I unfreeze that corridor scene, and in a moment the old Thinity's dead. Then it's happy ever after for you. Or,' he said, 'I could reset the scene there a little: take the bullets out of the Frurnchman's guns. I could let that Thinity live; and let you back through my wall to rejoin her. But she doesn't love you, and, the way she is – I'm sorry to say – she never will. That's just how it is.'

'Oh,' said Nemo, as the full force of the choice sank in.

'Like you said,' the Designer said, 'from *her* point of view, it'd be a death. But the new Thinity would be pretty much the same, as far as you were concerned.'

'Allow Thinity to die, so that I can be with her for ever,' said Nemo in a small voice. 'That's what the Orifice said to me.'

'Well, she's a bit mad. She's lived inside the McAtrix

for many thousands of years, and it's turned her wits a little. But she's basically a very clever and far-seeing person.'

'You're giving me the choice: to kill Thinity, so that I can have a rewired version to live with me and be my love. Or to let Thinity go on living, and doom myself to a lonely and miserable existence.'

'That's pretty much it.'

'How could I live with the guilt of knowing that I'd killed the woman I loved?'

'Well,' said the Designer, scratching his chin. 'I guess you'd have the actual Thinity, the real woman, with you – loving you, wanting you – so you could tell yourself that she isn't dead. And she wouldn't be dead; she'd be exactly as alive as you.'

'But that Thinity – the person living behind her eyes, out there,' said Nemo, pointing at the wall again. '*She* would die.'

'Believe me, her replacement would be exactly like her, except that she'd love you. If Thinity walked out of a room and walked back in exactly the same except that she loved you, would you complain? Would you mind? Would you care what had happened outside the room? Or would you just thank your good fortune?'

Nemo pondered. 'This is a horrible choice. If I really love Thinity, I should put her needs before mine, I should sacrifice myself for her sake. That's what love means. I can't kill her.'

'That's altruism, not love,' said Bill. 'Be realistic. Love is selfish. Love wants the loved person for itself. Lovers sometimes kill the people they love rather than lose them, don't they?'

'Psychos do, maybe,' retorted Nemo. 'But true love – true love, like the thing I feel for Thinity . . .'

Bill shrugged. 'Seems to me that love is a connection, and that without that connection it's not really love. So you could say your choice is: do you want Thinity to die, or do you want *your love* to die? What's actually more important to you?'

'How could I say I love a woman if I'm prepared to see her die for my own future gratification?'

'But she won't really die. Not from your point of view. She'll come back to life with all her abilities, and faculties, and thoughts.'

'But not her memories.'

'No. But she'll develop new memories. She'll be alive. From *your* point of view she'll be there, only loving you.'

'So what matters is *which* point of view I think is the important one. Hers or mine.'

'Ah,' said the Designer. 'You've hit it. Which point of view? That's what love boils down to, isn't it? I mean, if we're being honest. So – what's your decision? Which is it to be?'

'Oh,' said Nemo, looking from the Designer to the image of Thinity on the screen. 'Oh, God, oh. I don't know.'

'I'm going to have to press you,' said Bill, smiling. 'I really need your decision now.'

Epilogue

'So? What happened?'

They were back in the lobby. Through the glass doors they could see the street outside, sunshine paling the tarmac beyond the crenellated shadow silhouette of the rooftops. A mother pushed a pram up the street. A taxi barrelled down, brakes singing, paused at the junction and drove off again. On the opposite pavement a beggar held a copy of the *Big Issue* at arms' length, as if it were toxic. Three tourists were taking photographs of a red London Transport twenty-seven-horsepower omnibus. Thinity touched Nemo's arm. 'Nemo?' she said again. 'What happened?'

'He gave me a choice. The Designer.'

'A choice? What choice?'

'That's not so important. But I made my choice, and he let me leave his office, let me back into the McAtrix. I think he won't be bothering us any more. I think we can just get on with our lives now.'

'And what did you choose?'

Nemo swallowed. 'I chose what any person in my position would have chosen. Any sane person. Any person in love.'

Thinity looked at him. 'I really don't understand,' she said. 'You'll have to make yourself plainer.'

'Really,' Nemo replied. 'That's as plain as I can be. Come on, let's be on our way.' So Nemo and Thinity and Smurpheus stepped out of the building, and into the street outside.

Bonus Pages

The Making of
The McAtrix Derided

Special features.

• *Author's Commentary*

Press this button ⊕ for simultaneous commentary whilst you read

p.1. The first page. Actually it was the last page written. We'd been on this massive writing schedule, writing three chapters back to back – something never before attempted in the history of writing, actually – and at the end we sketched out the first page and wrote it straight down. Except for the 'and's. The 'and's were added later by *Industrial Estate Light and Magic*.

p.17. A very difficult page to write. Very difficult, technically speaking. But I wrote it, eventually.

p.25. I said to Tallulah and Banksie, 'I don't like the margins on p.25,' and they said, 'It's margin on the ridiculous,' which I thought was very funny. Very funny. They were a great team, it was always jokes and laughter with them.

p.51. Yeah.

p.90. There's a deliberate error on this page, an *ommage* to Hitchcock: if you take every third letter you spell out 'FRCHUHRMMA', which, sort of, sounds like 'Robertski Brothers' if you say it out loud.

p.99. Hey, man, I remember this! This was great!

p.127. This page was designed as a magic eye image; if you defocus your eyes as you look at all the words you're supposed to be able to see a picture of George W. Bush naked on the back of a heifer smoking a joint rolled out of the front page of the *New York Times*. It picked out the political subtext of the whole project. Sadly the printer inserted too many spaces after punctuation points, and the image was ruined. Now if you squinny up your eyes the most you can see is a naked Meryl Streep with the head of an auk sitting astride a piano player, which isn't nearly as political. It's still political, obviously. But just not *as* political.

p.173. Although it looks like this page is written in the Seychelles, in fact it was written in Middlesex. Actually – I know this is hard to believe – actually I was sitting in a little room in Middlesex, but I had this pot plant, and I turned the heating way way up and put on some Seychellese music. It's amazing how you can write in a way to disguise the actual stuff that gets written. Tricks of the trade.

p.179. During the writing of this page I had the publisher on the blower to me constantly, couldn't get him off my neck. 'You're going over budget on this page! You're going wildly over budget! We're pulling the plug . . .' Originally I planned to put 4,500 words on this page. Man, that would have been something! In the event the money men recalled the extras, and I had to make do with 350 words. But that's always the way when art clashes with commerce.

p.200. This was a three-cup-of-tea page.

p.211. Oh *man*!

Theatrical Trailer

THE McATRIX DERIDED – a Parody of The Matrix. BUY IT NOW!

TV Spots

BUY *THE McATRIX DERIDED!*

From all good bookstores

Bookseller Spot

Another parody from Gollancz: *The McAtrix Derided*, available May.

Guardian Ad

Also published: *The McAtrix Decided*, from Gollancz

Deleted Scenes
The Gordon Stops Off At A Starbucks For A Cup Of Coffee Before Catching His Train scene

On the way to the station to catch his morning train to work, Gordon stopped off at the Starbucks for a cup of coffee. He had plenty of time. He sat in the Starbucks and nursed his coffee for a while, staring out of the window, until it was cool enough to drink. Then he drank it, taking precise little sips and drawing it to the back of his mouth and down his gullet to his stomach. It not only tasted good to him, but it perked him up – the caffeine in the drink entering his bloodstream as a stimulant. As he sat in the Starbucks people came and went, some buying coffee in paper cups to carry away with them, some purchasing drinks in ceramic containers to consume on the premises. Eventually, his coffee drunk, Gordon left the emporium and went off to catch his train.

Alternate Ending

Gordon woke up – it had all been a dream. Fancy that, he thought to himself. Fancy that. Well, I've certainly learnt my lesson.

The McANImcATRIX

Six short stories set in the McAtrix universe

1. The Last Flight of the Papyrus

He was naked, except for a tight pair of jeans. Perfectly rendered sweatdrops stood out like glass pearls on the taut sculptured magnificence of his torso. He moved with fluid grace.

She was wearing the skimpiest of tops, the tiniest of pants. She possessed a pair of enormous, magically anti-gravitational breasts; endowments that not so much depended as suspended before her like helium-filled pink spheres, swaying and moving as she danced from side to side.

She demonstrated extraordinary facility with her swordplay, and extraordinary grace in her movements, but it was hard to pay attention to those achievements given the fantastic prominence of her breasts.

The two of them, man and woman, were fighting with swords. The sheen of light on the swords was glittery, glorious, and perfectly rendered. Any third party (although there were no other combatants there apart from the two gorgeously sexy people aforementioned) would have been struck by how fantastically lifelike it all looked. Vivid. Photorealistic.

Every downy hair on her body, every pore, was visible under the softly diffusing light. Every freckle on his face, every strand of his head hair, stood out. The grain of the wood of every beam was clearly discernible. The banners fluttered ever so slightly in the air.

The man's sword sliced through the air, passing the woman's flesh by nanoinches. A cut appeared in the silk of her pants.

With aching slowness the silk slipped from her hips and fell to the floor. Beneath the panties she was wearing a thong. Her pert, perfectly shaped bottom was revealed in its globular glory.

The man looked, appreciatively, at the woman.

She swung her own sword, and—

– abruptly, there came a voice over the intercom. 'Come quickly!' somebody yelled. 'We are under attack by creatures in the real world.'

'The real world,' gasped the woman.

Quickly they exited the luminous virtual realm in which they had been fighting, and, let's be honest, *stripteasing* one another. Don't ask me why. Perhaps striptease is an important military tool in this future-age war against the machines. It doesn't make a lot of sense to me, but then I'm only the narrator. *I* don't know. Perhaps the ability to remove all one's clothes slowly whilst carrying a sword is highly prized by the generals. Perhaps if the Carthaginian army had tried that tactic then they wouldn't have been defeated by Scipio Africanus and his Roman legions. Perhaps Napoleon's troops would have conquered the *whole* of Russia if they'd been wearing thongs and been prepared to show the enemy that fact. I mean – come *on*, this is a training program, this is supposed to be training up the human army in their fighting skills. But there you go.

Anyway, no rest for the narrator, I'd better tell you the rest of the story. So they rush up to the cockpit, or brig, or whatever they call it, but here it's all pretty murky and sketchy. Not much light, you see. Not that I'm suggesting that, after blowing their budget on the swordfight-striptease hyperreal section the directors had no money for more detail than vague squirmy shapes and a couple of explosions. Not at all. But, as narrator, it's a little tricky for me to be exact – some fighting, shooting at attacking SQUIDS, explosions, and it all ends tragically. If I were you I'd go back to the opening paragraphs with the two beautiful semi-naked people prancing around.

2. McAtrix Ghost Story

Pretty much a regular ghost story, only it turns out that the ghost is actually a malfunction in the logic of the McAtrix.

3. McAtrix Vampire Story

Once again, this is pretty much your basic vampire story, only it turns out that the vampire is actually a malfunction in the logic of the McAtrix. You see? Clever, isn't it? By using this same explanation the creators of the McAtrix can rationalise almost any supernatural or unusual tale they like.

4. McAtrix UFO Story

Well, I'm assuming you've got the hang of the basic premise here.

5. McAtrix Chicklit

Sally works in a boring office job and has no luck with men, until one week she cops off with *two* handsome and wealthy blokes at the office party! Follow her hilarious adventures through one event-packed week whilst she tries to balance friends, work, love and laughter before eventually settling down and marrying a malfunction in the logic of the McAtrix.

6. What Not To Wear in the McAtrix

Transistor and Su-Circuit show what the clued-in silicon chip is wearing this season. *Out* go flares, colour, shirts, sweaters, loafers, kaftans, hats, brown suede waistcoats and jeans, and *in* come black suits, white shirts, sunglasses and National Health hearing aids.

**Also available in the Victor Gollums *SF Masterpieces
Cheaper Than Commissioning New Novels Reprint* Series**

Build your Science Fiction Library with these essential
SF Masterpieces:

Dung
by Francis 'Dip' Sherbert

In the year 468,579, the family Atrydeezbutinolikedem
leave their home planet to make a new life for themselves
on the world of Arrantpis, also known as 'Dung', a planet
whose entire surface is wholly covered by ordure. Duke
Jonwain Atrydeezbutinolikedem is assassinated by Sheriff
Fatman; and the Duke's young son Paulie Atrydeezbutinolikedem has no choice but to flee into the deserts of
Dung. The landscape is not pleasant, and the imperial
citizens (who all live inside the hermetically sealed and
extensively deoderised Pod City) consider it utterly
insupportable of life, so much so that Sheriff Fatman
gives up his pursuit of Paulie, convinced that he must be
dead. But Paulie survives by pinching his nose, and not
thinking too precisely about what he is walking through,
and is eventually rescued by the native Dungians, the
Pheuweemen. Eventually he is accepted by these simple
but brave (obviously) people, and is recognised as the

Mud-Dibbyk, the saviour prophesied by their religion. He comes to understand the precise relationship between the mile-long Tapeworms that live under the surface of this strange world and the Tomatoes that grow only there, and are prized throughout the galaxy.

'A masterpiece. I had to take three showers after finishing reading it before I started to feel clean.'

Clarke 'Kent' Arthur.

Also available:

Dung Messier
Children's Nappies of Dung
God-Awful Smell of Dung
Hairy Ticks of Dung
Champignons Housed in Dung

Nerdomancer
by William 'Wild Bill' Hiccough-Gibson

In Hiccough-Gibson's famous near-future dystopia, Casey is a cutting-edge info-hacker, a man who spends almost all his life programming, playing with, dismantling, rebuilding and hacking into computers. Then one day the beautiful leather-clad Maggie presents him with the offer of a lifetime: if he can hack into the Snark-guarded virtual world of Megacorps and rescue one particular mcguffin, then the two of them will be rich beyond the virtual dreams of avarice. 'So whaddaya say, bright boy?' she asks him. 'You in?' Casey, as you'd expect, adjusts his sunglasses on the bridge of his nose with his index finger, and calls out, 'Mom? *Mo-o-om*? Can Maggie stay for supper? I'll be online for only a couple more hours – if you bring us up some pizza and Doctor Peppers and maybe some coo-*oo*-ookies?' And, from downstairs, his mother calls up, 'Casey you've been on that computer long enough, I think, you remember what Doctor Kugelman said about keeping your weight down, about eating greens and getting a little exercise, two hundred thirty pounds is just *too much* for someone your age. And you *promised* me – no more hacking, of any kind. All right, sweetie? I'll bring you and your friend some lemonade and apples if you like.' And Casey says, 'Awww . . . *Mom*!' There's pretty much three hundred pages of that. But, what can I tell you: it's computers. *You* try and make computers, and the people who live and breathe them, sexy or interesting.

The Invisible Man
by H. G. 'Ill' Wells

The timeless classic. Wells's evil scientist invents a ray that renders him invisible, a power which he plans to use to take over the world, ruthlessly tricking and murdering his way to the top. Laughing maniacally, he places himself in the path of the ray, and becomes invisible to the naked eye. Sadly his own naked eye is one of the organs rendered invisible, such that his retina is no longer able to register the light that strikes it. Accordingly he stumbles about completely blind, banging into walls, walking into lamp-posts, tripping over small dogs and falling down open manholes.

Read all the sequels in the complete '*H. G. Wells's Invisible Man*' series:

- Son of Invisible Man
- The Invisible Woman
- The Invisible Dog
- The Invisible Frankenstein Meets Invisible Abbot and Invisible Costello
- Invisible Invertebrates
- Invisible Invertebrates 2: Invisible Invertebrates Invade
- Invisible Invertebrates 3: The Return of Invisible Invertebrates
- The Invisible Tailor Makes Clothes for the Emperor
- Invisible Book.*

* You may already have this book on your shelves. To be honest, it's pretty hard to be sure one way or another.

The Leather Handkerchief of Darkness
by Lester le Gurn

Gently Ow, diplomat from the Central Galactic Administration, visits the unique world of Gachoo, a planet on which everybody has a cold all the time. He sneezes, groans, sniffs, shivers and goes bleary-eyed in an attempt to persuade the Gachooians to join the CGA, before eventually giving up.

The Man in the High Chair
by Flippy Penis

Penis's Alternate History won the Nebulous Award for 'Best Sort-Of Book, Kinda SF-y, We Like It Anyhow' of 1967. It is set in a timeline in which Hitler won the Second World War, and America is divided between the Nazis in the east and the Visigoths in the west (a slightly confused timeline, to be honest). In this world Gilbert Fah, the 'Man in the High Chair' of the title, writes an SF alternate history called *The Cricket Squats*, set in a world in which *America* won the Second World War. The main character in this novel is a medium called Jim who receives messages from an alternate reality in which *Hitler* won the Second World War. The individual from whom the medium receives the messages, Madox, is a film director in his own dimension, making a movie set in a fantasy world where

America won the Second World War. Madox's movie is about a group of female close-harmony singers who release a concept album set in a world in which *Hitler* won the Second World War. The third song on this album [cont. p.293]

(Publishers' note: this Gollum Masterpiece Reissue comes complete with an appendix by a famous historian that reminds readers who it was who actually won the Second World War. So far as we can tell.)

Flash
by Merry Gentile

In this epic, 4,700-page retelling of the Flash Gordon story (the single largest one-volume novel booksellers have been prepared to unpack from their boxes and lug upstairs to the shop shelves)* award-winning author Merry Gentile has created something unique. Her 'Flash' grows up a discarded waif on a military camp of the army of Myng the Non-Merci. A girl in a man's world, she disguises herself as 'Gor Don', a honed fighting machine (with a university education), to survive. Accordingly she rises through the

* There was a Peter Hamilton novel that ran to 5,150 pages, but the booksellers refused to handle it without heavy-lifting equipment and so it never made the shelves.

ranks until she is able to lead an army against the thankless Myng; and yet – her tragedy – she cannot wholly purge her masculine persona of feminine attributes. Her followers start to suspect that her various camp mannerisms, the gaudy decorations she prefers, the extremely clean spaceships she insists upon and her general attention to detail are incompatible with the rough, crude, belly-scratching world of men fighting wars with other men in a manly way. And so the book moves, not hurriedly, towards its tragic climax.

'I started reading this novel in 2001, and I have found it impossible to put down. I am absorbed in it every night before I go to sleep, I keep a copy in the toilet, take it on the train with me, and spend my weekends immersed in it. I hope to finish it by 2007.' *Martin Amis.*

Fundament
by Isaac Maseltov

The millions worlds of the Cosmic Imperium have lasted for thousands of years, and its decadent population assume it will last for thousands more. Only the psycho historian Hairy Shelgoon can foresee the inevitability of its collapse. Accordingly, he creates the Fundament on the planet Gluteus Minimus: an organisation devoted to preserving the memory of True Civilisation for future generations by writing a multi-volume *Hitchhikers' Encyclopedia of the Galaxy*. Work on this great work proceeds whilst the Cosmic Imperium does indeed collapse: it gives the people of the galaxy hope, with the *Encyclopedia* becoming for many a sacred work. But then the compilers of the *Guide* become distracted by writing piffling detective-agency novels, undertaking rainforest conservation projects, CD-ROMS about the *Titanic*, appearances on *Parkinson* and *Wogan*, articles in computer magazines about slight improvements to user-interfaces, and the like. Tragically, the great *Hitchhikers' Encyclopedia of the Galaxy* is unfinished, and civilisation is unable to function properly without it. Woe.

The remaining titles in the 'Fundament' trilogy:

Second Fundament
Up Your Fundament

The second trilogy:

Cream of Foundation
Garment of Foundation
Al-Qaeda of Foundation

The third, or 'cash-in' trilogy:

Foundation, Robots, Time Travel, and Everything I've
Ever Written About Are All Part of the Same Universe,
Difficult As That May Be To Believe
Forsythias for the Foundation
Fortepianos of the Foundation

The fourth or 'not even written by him' trilogy:

Footlings of the Foundation
Forty Winks with the Foundation
Four-poster time for the Foundation

The fifth, or 'oh you cannot be serious' trilogy:

Fortissimo, Foundation!
Foundate, Foundation!
The Fourteen Fountains of Forever (Foundation 15)

Chairlifts of the Gods

by Erich von Donut Dunkin

Was Earth colonised forty thousand years ago by a decrepit
race of gerontaliens, who sculpted the landscape to make it
easier to get from the bedroom to the kitchen? Is Stone-
henge a picnic table for an alien day trip? Is Tower Bridge
an aerial for picking up intergalactic afternoon hypervision

programmes such as *Rocketlaunch Countdown* and *Murder She Wrote in Undecipherable Hieroglyphs Engraved upon a Mysterious Artefact made of Hitherto Unknown Metal*?

Obviously no.

Also available: the sequels: *How Wrong I Was: No Spacemen in Earth's History At All*, and *Boy Is My face Red, I Made Up Most of my Evidence*.

The Second Mars Trilogy
by Stan Lee Kim-il-Sung Robinsonade

Three enormous books that continue the saga begun with Robinsonade's original Mars Trilogy.

Mars 4. Purple Mars. Something goes very wrong with the terraforming of Mars, and a purple haze descends over everything, all in my brain as well as all over the planet. What's that? Terraforming, yes. That's what I said. All right, all right, 'areoforming', *phhw*, if you're really so pedantically minded – for crying out loud, who cares? Areoforming, schmareoforming. Terraforming is the *general* noun covering all such cases. That's right. That's my position, and I'm sticking to it.

Mars 5. Lime Mars with Regularly Spaced Dark Brown Circles. An alien race whose only contact with Earth civilisation consists of a brief window of 1970s design magazines that accidentally fell through a wormhole in the etc. etc. arrive and remake Mars in what they assume are colours humanity will applaud.

Mars 6. Beige Mars. Many thousands of years in the future posthumans revisit Mars and alter it so it conforms with what is now considered the most beautiful colour in the cosmos.

What Hologram, Jeeves!
by Pee Jee Woodenspaceships

The classic comedy.

> 'Comedy' – *Breamwatch: Fish-Fanciers Monthly*
> 'Classic' – *SFZ* 'The' – *Prepositions Quarterly and Digest*

New From
Victor Gollums Video

Sighs
Directed by M. Night Shamalamalamalamalamalamadingdong
Starring: Mel Gibbon, Joachimp Primate, Ann Ape

The chilling SF classic. Alien creatures who are by their nature intensely allergic to water (to the point where water acts upon their body much as sulphuric acid acts upon human flesh) decide to invade Earth – a planet where water lies around on the surface in vast pools, where water vapour hangs densely in the air at almost every latitude, and water falls regularly out of the sky. They land and parade about our world wearing no protective clothing of any kind. They are easily defeated.

It later transpires that these aliens were inmates of a galactic lunatic asylum who had been out on a day trip to Ursa Minor when their minder had popped into a space toilet to relieve himself and they'd wandered off unsupervised. Their fate causes galactic outrage, and Earth is shunned by the more civilised alien races for picking on such obviously harmless cretins.

'Fun whilst it lasts. However afterwards, when you think about it, it makes prodigiously little sense.'

Imperial Film Magazine

Apollo 14
Dir: Ron Howard

In this sequel to his Oscar-winning smash hit *Apollo 13*, Howard returns to the world of 1970s space exploration. The film follows the launch of Apollo 14, its uneventful three-day voyage through space, its successful landing on the moon, its astronauts collecting rocks, driving about in a car made of knitting needles and wire mesh, collecting some more rocks, eating processed food in their module, going out to collect some more rocks, planting a flag with a wire support along the top edge to make the cloth stand up in the vacuum, picking up some more rocks, and then flying home safely and without incident.

'Perhaps the most boring science fiction film every made' –
Rock Collectors Monthly

'I used to be in *Happy Days*, you know' –   Ron Howard

Blade Runner

Dir: Scott 'Scotty' Scott

An evil scientist creates a matter-transference machine, into which he puts (*a*) a movie about two guys (or 'blade runners') smuggling medical supplies and scalpels into 1980s Latin America, and (*b*) another movie about an 'android hunter' hunting androids in a far-future dystopia. He presses the button, and at the other end emerges a monstrous mutated combination of the two – a film with a title that bears no relationship *at all* to its subject matter.

Do you dare to view the resulting hybrid freak? Do you *dare* sit through it with friends, drinking beer and eating potato chips, to face their puzzled questions afterwards, 'So why *was* it called *Blade Runner* then? Where were the Blades? Did I miss something?'? Do you *dare* to find Rutger Hauer strangely arousing, even though you're straight, honestly you are, no, really, although it's true that those builders whistled at you last time you walked past that building site, although perhaps that was more sort-of taking the piss, now that you come to think of it?

Also available: the soundtrack: *Blade Runner, Music By Mintgellies*.

'If your idea of good music is early 1980s synths and somebody wailing in the background very slowly, then this will appeal to you.' – *MNMNME*

Blade 3: The Runner
Dir: Scott 'Scotty' Scott

In *Blade* you were awed by the high-octane action adventures as Wesley Schnaps hunted evil vampires. In *Blade 2*, you were staggered by the even higher-octane adventures, as Schnaps became caught in an eon-long war in which vampire-vampires preyed on regular vampires. Now, in *Blade 3: The Runner*, prepare to have your socks blown *quite literally* off your feet as Wesley Schnaps encounters vampire-vampire-vampires, specialist predators who prey only on the vampires who prey on ordinary vampires. As with any pyramidic food chain, there are only a very few of these vampire-vampire-vampires about, but they're pretty scary, believe you me, so scary that Schnaps's character spends most of the movie running away from them.

Blade 4: Sheffield Wednesday
Dir: Scott 'Scotty' Scott

In this latest instalment in the *Blade* vampire saga, Hulk 'The Budget Didn't Run To Wesley Schnaps' Hogan comes up against humanity's most terrifying adversaries yet: vampires that feed only on vampires that prey on vampires that feed on regular vampires. There are only a very, very few of these beings in the world, eleven in total, and they masquerade as the Sheffield Wednesday first squad to avoid the spotlight of publicity.

Solaris: the Musical
Dir: Tarkovsky the Otter

Astronauts go very, very slowly mad in space, whilst a planet (very, very, very slowly) turns out to be some kind of brain, with chirpy musical-comedy interludes. Includes the songs: 'So, a Laris, a Female Laris', Smokey Robinson's 'Tears of a Clooney', 'I Want To Teach the World to Appreciate-Human-Culture-during-a-First-Encounter-with-Alien-Life', 'Natty Little Solaris With a Fri-ii-inge On Top' and many others.

'Perhaps the most boring science fiction film every made' –
Rock Collectors Monthly

¡Special Offers
to Readers of
The McAtrix Derided!

McAtrix Sunglasses – *just like Smurpheus's!*

In our sweatshops in East Cheam, teams of poorly paid workers are, even as we speak, taking £1.99 bulk-bought regular sunglasses, snapping off their two supporting arms, tossing those into big bins and putting what's left over into silvery boxes with 'THE MCATRIX DERIDED' written on the front. Now you can by the resulting Cool Shades, at a special MCATRIX DERIDED introductory offer of £49.99 a pair.

Look Just Like Smurpheus! Buy One Today! Buy A Couple! Go On!

Also available:
McAtrix-style Mobile Phone
Personally endorsed by Elfrond 'the Agent' Warping

Elfrond says: 'The life of an internationally famous antipodean film star with a receding hairline is a hectic one. Accordingly I never travel anywhere without my **Mobile Palantir™**. Be like me! Keep up with the Smiths! Get a **Mobile Palantir™** of your own!'

All **Mobile Palantir™** are constructed using *only* the finest polished stone globes, and fit snugly in any pocket, pouch, or wrapped in black silk and tucked neatly into your robe. Whether on foot, horseback or kick-boxing a Hong Kong-trained martial arts expert, nothing is more convenient than whipping out a **Mobile Palantir™**, waving your hand over the top of it in an arthritic sort of shape, and summoning the image of the person with whom you wish to speak.

Ordinary phone companies promise you tomorrow's communication technology today; but only we guarantee you *yesterday's communication device tomorrow*, or the day after tomorrow (leave fourteen days for delivery) (so, technically, that's the day after the day after the day after the day after the day after the day after the day after the day after the day after the day after the day after the day after tomorrow).

NOTE: Mobile Palantir plc (Palantir Limited Company) accept no responsibility for loss of mind due to crossed lines leading to a vision of ultimate evil, the violent destruction of your hometown, or broken bones resultant from dropping one on your foot. 'Mobile', 'Palantir' and 'plc' are all registered trade marks.

Meet The 'Internet'!
Why Not?

Have you enjoyed *The McAtrix Derided*? Do you want to learn more about the sinister power of 'the internet', 'machinic intelligences', 'processing technology' and the like? Then why not visit

The 'Internet'!

You don't need a 'passport' to visit the 'Internet' . . . so make the journey today!*

Here are just some of the dozens of websites you may enjoy:
Like legs? Lovely!
www.legs-and.co.uk and www.morethantheaveragenumberofpenis-es.com. Do you have two legs? Conratulations!† Since a small portion of the general population has only one leg (and some have

---

* You do, however, need a computer, modem and phone link, which, if I'm honest, costs more than a passport. But if you're 'poor', then why not *not* visit the internet, but just go abroad instead? It's not as good, but it's probably better than sitting around at home feeling sorry for yourself.

† Note: there are typographical errors on some 'internet' pages.

no legs at all) it follows logically that the average number of legs in the population as a whole is less than two. This means that you possess *more than the average number of legs*. Strange, eh? The same inescapable logic also applies to ears, eyes, arms, nostrils, and, if you are a man, genitals. Indeed, the *average number* of penises in the world as a whole is *less than 0.5*, which means that most men can boast that they possess *more than twice the average number of penises*. Which can only be a good thing. Can't it? Hey ho.

Pongy

deoderant.de, the German Oderant Website, is the place you'll find a scratch-screen-and-sniff of Germany's Favourite Cat-related Smells.

Interestingly, the acronym for this site 'GOW' came top of the Readers' Poll vote 2003 chart at www.Singlesyallablewordsthat-don'tmeananythingbutreallyoughtto.com just ahead of 'MUP' and 'HENG'.

KKK!

Check out the Karate Kid sequels page www.KingKarateKid.com on which dedicated fans have posted their complete shooting scripts for as-yet-unmade Karate Kid sequels, including 'Karate Thirty-something III' by Nick Adsell, 'Karate Middle Age Man' by Hannah Voelspiet and 'Karate Kid Senior Citizen: Prostate Op IV' by Kevin 'Kid' Keegan.